Shadow Lane
Volume 4

The Chronicles of Random Point

by
Eve Howard

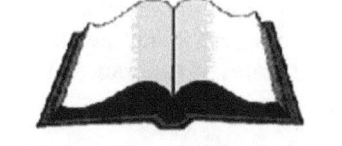

CCB Publishing
British Columbia, Canada

Shadow Lane Volume 4: The Chronicles of Random Point,
Spanking, Sex, B&D and Anal Eroticism in a Small New England Village

Copyright ©2009 by Eve Howard
ISBN-13 978-1-926585-31-4
Second Edition

Library and Archives Canada Cataloguing in Publication
Howard, Eve, 1953-
Shadow lane volume 4: the chronicles of random point, spanking, sex, b&d and
anal eroticism in a small New England village / written by Eve Howard – 2nd ed.
ISBN 978-1-926585-31-4
Also available in electronic format.
I. Title.
PS3608.O82S534 2009   813'.6   C2009-903095-0

Cover artwork by Tarsis: www.briantarsis.com

Shadow Lane Volume 4 was first published by Blue Moon in 1998,
Copyright © Eve Howard.

Publisher: CCB Publishing
               British Columbia, Canada
               www.ccbpublishing.com

Dedicated to

Stephanie Locke

Shadow Lane

Volume 4

The Chronicles of Random Point,
Spanking, Sex, B&D and Anal Eroticism
in a Small New England Village

Contents

Chapter One

Miss Oliver
(A Retrospective Random Point Story)

One Friday afternoon in the early autumn of 1958, sunny Miss Oliver, who taught first grade at The Crescent Elementary school in Random Point, Massachusetts, was walking towards the teachers' lounge with the amiable Mr. Johanson, who taught sixth grade, when both were witness to a small scene in the second floor corridor involving the strict, third grade teacher Miss Kranz and two of her female pupils. The little girls hugged the corridor wall, looking up at Miss Kranz with abject terror as she took turns shaking them by the shoulders and demanding to know what they meant by spitting at each other in her classroom.

"But we were just saying 'petunia,'" one of the children tried to explain.

"Never mind that, you're both disgusting!" accused the very thin and stylish Miss Kranz.

It upset Miss Oliver to see a child scolded, no less manhandled, and she averted her gaze. But Mr. Johanson gave Miss Oliver a long, hard look, as they passed, not bothering to conceal his disapproval of her manner.

"I want you to put your tablets on my desk, girls. I'm writing you both notes home," said Miss Kranz to the trembling children.

"Yes, Miss Kranz," the two frightened girls replied and ran back into their classroom.

Once they were well beyond the classroom of Miss Kranz, Mr. Johanson scowled, "What makes that girl so mean?"

"Do you think she's really mean?" Miss Oliver didn't like to think badly of anyone.

"One of those little girls' father has an awful temper and will probably spank her tonight when she gives him that note to sign."

Miss Oliver felt a queer little thrill ripple through her core when Mr. Johanson mentioned spanking. She'd felt the sensation before, particularly while watching certain episodes of I Love Lucy and Wagon Train, and was certain that her own interest in the subject of spanking was naughty and possibly not to be shared with anyone. (Unless they brought it up first, as Mr. Johanson had.)

"Don't you approve of spanking, Mr. Johanson?" Miss Oliver asked daringly.

"Oh, enthusiastically, but only for adults," he replied, thinking how badly Miss Kranz needed one.

"I'd love to see you spank that naughty Miss Kranz!" Miss Oliver giggled, accepting a cup of tea, which Mr. Johanson prepared for her in the lounge. "You'd probably do a very good job with those strong, pianist's hands," she added ingenuously, for Mr. Johanson was considered the most gifted musician on the faculty.

"I wish you were the naughty one, Miss Oliver," Mr. Johanson mused. "You'd be fun to spank!"

"Me?" Miss Oliver blushed all over and hid her confusion by lighting a cigarette. She wore a white blouse, a light grey cashmere cardigan over her shoulders and a charcoal wool straight skirt. Her pumps were high enough to feel best when she removed them, but they set off her elegant legs to perfection. Miss Oliver had creamy white skin, a long, high, blonde ponytail and a 24" waist. Taken all together, she was far too young and lovely for Mr. Johanson to flirt with, but for the fact that he had never felt so attracted to a girl in his life.

Miss Oliver was only 24, fresh from graduate school and in command of her very first class. Mr. Johanson was 38, had been teaching at Crescent for 15 years and was thought by all of his associates to be a confirmed bachelor.

"Yes, you, Miss Oliver. Why, you're probably the most spankable girl I know."

"Me?" she laughed again. "Why?"

"Because you're so cute."

"I could be naughtier, Mr. Johanson," she suggested flirtatiously.

"You wouldn't know how to if you tried, Miss Oliver."

"I am tediously well behaved, aren't I?" she lamented. "It's always been that way with me, Mr. Johanson."

"Don't feel badly about it, Miss Oliver. You're going to make some lucky man a splendid wife some day."

"Oh, I'm not sure I'm going to get married," she told him seriously.

"Not get married?" Mr. Johanson had never heard such a statement from a young schoolteacher before.

"Oh no, Mr. Johanson. I believe in free love," Miss Oliver replied.

"I see! Miss Oliver is progressive, even radical. I suppose that on the weekends you migrate to the coffee houses of Boston to listen to beat poetry and jazz?"

"How did you know? Do you like beat poetry, Mr. Johanson?"

"Indeed I do, Miss Oliver."

Miss Oliver waited for him to speak again.

"Miss Oliver?"

"Yes, Mr. Johanson?"

"Perhaps we could go into Boston together some weekend to listen to jazz."

"Oh, Mr. Johanson, that would be so wonderful! Sometimes when I go alone I get approached by the most inappropriate people and I don't know how to get rid of them."

"They've probably guessed your views on marriage."

"You think so?"

"Don't all girls who hang around coffee houses share those views?"

"I don't know. I never manage to talk to any girls," she reflected. "But many of my classmates at college did."

Mr. Johanson looked at the clock and saw it was time for them to claim their classes from recess in the schoolyard. They walked out together and continued to talk, this time about Charlie Parker and Miles Davis.

"What a splendid girl," thought Mr. Johanson as he watched Miss

Oliver walk across the yard to find her little ones. Miss Oliver turned to wave at him, and in turning back, walked into Mr. Albrecht, the stern Vice Principal. Mr. Albrecht was in his middle thirties, lean, sandy-haired, nattily suited for a man in his position and handsome in spite of his perpetually unsmiling visage. He terrified all young children.

"Careful, young lady!" he scolded, deftly sidestepping a full force collision with Miss Oliver.

"Oh, I beg your pardon, Mr. Albrecht," cried Miss Oliver, blushing with embarrassment.

"That's all right, Miss Oliver," he replied, a fraction of a smile tugging at the corners of his thin lips for an instant before he continued across the yard.

"That man would be so much more attractive if he'd only smile now and then," thought Miss Oliver, gathering her class into two lines and shepherding them back into the school building.

If Miss Kranz was Mr. Johanson's least favorite faculty member, Mr. Albrecht was certainly Miss Oliver's. She hated the way he bullied the little boys, dragging them into the bathroom and roughing them up to frighten them. Miss Oliver had no idea what Mr. Albrecht did to the little boys in the bathroom, but she suspected it involved some form of corporal punishment. She didn't think that it was spanking; Mr. Albrecht's was more the shake-and-slap type.

Once Miss Oliver had been both shocked and ashamed to see Mr. Albrecht pick a little boy up by his ears for violating the no-talking rule during a fire drill. She had never seen a child's face get so red. She wondered what she would do if Mr. Albrecht ever dared to lay his hands on one of her small charges. Indeed, she knew that she would not allow it. To his credit, she had never seen him concern himself with the behavior or discipline of little girls. To be sure, there was no need as little girls always behaved flawlessly in his dread presence.

Miss Oliver resolved to discuss Mr. Albrecht in great detail with Mr. Johanson when they were alone in the city. A delicious thrill ran through her as she remembered Mr. Johanson's flirtatious remarks about spanking.

"I'll bet I could get him to spank me one of these days!" thought

Miss Oliver, while she put the children in their cots for their nap. Then she sat down at her piano in the back of the room to pick music for the day's singing lesson. As Miss Oliver picked out three simple songs, she reflected upon how beautifully Mr. Johanson played the piano. It wasn't everyone who could play Gershwin's Concerto in F. The sound of his piano wafted intoxicatingly out the windows of his fourth floor classroom every lunchtime.

"Imagine Mr. Johanson knowing about the beat poets!" Miss Oliver reflected, putting on her smock for finger-painting. "He is truly a man of many abilities," Miss Oliver thought. "And he isn't all that old. It's just those dowdy clothes he wears. I wish I could do something about that!"

Miss Oliver had very little personal experience of spanking. She had received a few spankings from her father as a child, but thought of these as scary and humiliating rather than exciting. The kind of spanking that interested her the most was the kind she saw in movies and on TV, where a handsome man spanked a grown-up lady. Just seeing a wonderful movie spanking was enough to make Miss Oliver flushed and restless for weeks.

Miss Oliver often fantasized about spanking before she went to sleep at night. She was not a virgin. She had a boyfriend in high school, a boyfriend in college and another in graduate school. She had been a free thinker since reading the autobiography of Isadora Duncan at age thirteen and did enjoy making love. But she didn't fantasize about it the way she did about spanking, which seemed so much more delightful.

Once or twice she got one of the boyfriends to spank her, but the resultant experience had been somehow lacking. Miss Oliver wanted a man who would think of spanking her naturally, like in the movies. Mr. Johanson seemed as though he might be that kind of wonderful man. He seemed to share her opinion that spanking was cute and enjoyable. Or at least he spoke as though he did.

When Miss Oliver had taken over the first grade class from Mrs. Sampson, the retiring teacher had told Miss Oliver not to forget the tradition of giving birthday spankings in front of the class. But Miss Oliver could not bring herself to ever implement the tradition herself, because her own feelings about spanking were so strong. She longed to communicate about her fixation to someone who might understand and sympathize, and wondered if Mr. Johanson might be a good choice.

Mr. Johanson was the cleverest teacher on the faculty and always taught the sixth grade honors class. He was witty and well read, informed on all current events and full of amusing anecdotal knowledge of the past. Of the men she knew, Peter Johanson seemed the most open-minded and flexible. But there was also a quaint, old-fashioned quality about him, from the sprinkling of grey in his temples to the throbbing pulse of Tin Pan Alley that sprung from his nimble fingers when he sat down at the upright in the back of his class. There were 14 years between them, but when he smiled and his blue eyes crinkled, she saw the boy was still alive in the man. However, she greatly disapproved of his moustache and did not scruple to tell him so after three or four innocent dates.

Peter had invited Jessie to dinner at his cottage on Lilac Cove. He himself had prepared their meal, which was a good deal more savory than if she had done so. In fact, Jessie blushed when she regarded the perfect serving of Chicken Kiev and pilaf on her plate, remembering the macaroni and cheese casserole she'd presented him the previous week in her apartment in the village.

It was very romantic, here on the cove, with the pounding surf so close. They dined by candlelight and Peter opened a good bottle of wine. Jessie was thrilled by these cultivated attentions. The wine went quickly to her head and sex, rendering her reckless and aroused.

"You know, Peter, you'd look ever so much more youthful without that horrid old moustache," she blurted out, shocking even herself with these words.

Peter was taken aback. And to think that tonight of all nights he was going to try to kiss her for the first time!

"So you don't like my moustache, eh?" Peter pretended that he wasn't hurt.

"It makes you look like William Powell."

"I thought it looked rather distinguished," he returned, clearing the table.

"That's just the problem. You're too young to look distinguished."

"I'm afraid I'm not very young at all," he smiled, going out of the room with the dishes. She scooped up several plates and followed him into the kitchen.

"I want to help."

"Very well," he told her, opening up his perfectly organized linen closet and getting out a chef's apron. "Let's see how you look in this," he slipped it over her head and turned her around to tie the bow in back. When he was done he gave her one light pat on the bottom. "Okay, get to work!"

Jessie quickly busied herself at the deep, old-fashioned sink to hide her fierce blush. The little smack stayed with her for many minutes, causing her to flush again and again, while her tummy contracted with pleasure.

No more was said about the moustache and no kiss was attempted. Jessie sat quietly by the window looking at the cove while Peter played for several hours, a troubled frown creasing his brow every now and then.

The next date they had was for Halloween, which fell on a Friday. Peter had made reservations for dinner in Woodbridge at an inn and later they were going to the revival movie house to see a double feature of Frontier Gal and The Wax Museum.

The movies had been Jessie's idea, after she chanced to see the lobby cards for Frontier Gal the previous week while shopping in the neighboring coastal town. One of the cards pictured the spanking of beautiful Yvonne de Carlo across the knee of handsome Rod Cameron, and all Jessie had been thinking of the whole week was how delightful it would be to watch just that kind of movie with dear Peter.

Jessie arrived at school that morning thinking that she had never felt so happy in her young life as on that splendid, golden autumn day. She was wearing a dove grey fitted wool dress and matching cropped jacket with a white linen collar. Her brand new light grey gloves, pumps and purse were all of suede and bore the label of Saks Fifth Avenue. Underneath all of this elegance were a charming little corselet and silk panties. For tonight of all nights, she cherished hopes of being unwrapped by her gentlemanly escort.

The moment she entered the schoolyard to assemble her class she looked for Peter, just as she had done so every morning for several weeks. She saw him right away across the yard and waved, then turned back to her class with the impression that something was different about him today.

It wasn't until the morning recess break that she got a closer look at Peter and realized that he had shaved his moustache and now seemed to look a lot more like Dick than William Powell. All at once she could see his face for the charming face that it was, not the prematurely middle aged one he had made it. Jessie noticed he had also gotten a sharp haircut, had his shoes shined and even seemed to have brushed his jacket that morning.

Jessie wasn't able to talk to Peter until lunchtime, when she found him sitting under a tree with his paper bag lunch spread out on the bench beside him. She had brought her own brown bag and added its contents to his.

"Peter, I'm overwhelmed that you took my criticism so seriously and shaved your moustache. How long did you have it?"

"Too long, Jessie. I was in a rut and you were right to point it out," he patted her hand fondly.

"You look ever so much more attractive now, Peter," she said, abandoning her plain cheese sandwich for one of the delicate tuna salad sandwich quarters he had prepared. "Mmmmm! You really know how to prepare food!" she murmured appreciatively, causing Peter to glow.

"The capers make all the difference," he explained.

Jessie gazed at him and smiled, more than pleased at the change, which the shaving had wrought. Was it possible she had really been seeing this handsome man for weeks without the exchange of one single kiss or squeeze? Jessie hoped that his admirable housekeeping and culinary acquirements were not symptoms of latent homosexuality.

"Now you get to change something about me," Jessie suggested.

"I wouldn't change an atom."

"How gallant, Peter. Some people don't share that feeling," Jessie said meaningfully.

"People like who?"

"Oh, horrid Mr. Albrecht. I inadvertently flicked him in the face with my ponytail while I was straightening up from the water fountain today."

"Oh dear, and what did he say?"

"He said I was too old to be wearing a ponytail and that it wasn't appropriate for a teacher anyway."

"Hateful man. I love your ponytail."

"I'm going to have to pin my hair up from now on."

"No!"

"Just during school hours," Jessie smiled.

It was at this pleasant juncture Mr. Albrecht strode past the two teachers on his way back to the school building. He nodded briskly to them both and looked thoughtful as he proceeded on his way.

Lionel Albrecht had been watching Miss Oliver ever since the semester began and wondered whether she was available for extracurricular activities. Now that she was apparently beginning to warm up to Mr. Johanson of all people, Lionel's vigorous and competitive libido began to send messages to his brain to make a move. The notion of losing the precious Miss Oliver to Mr. Johanson irritated the Vice Principal. And never more so than when he overheard them making plans to meet that evening for their date.

It seemed to Lionel that the only possible reason a girl like Miss Oliver would consent to date a fossil like Mr. Johanson was loneliness. Therefore he resolved not to waste another moment before inviting her out himself.

Lionel found an opportunity to speak with Miss Oliver during afternoon recess in the schoolyard. Pausing on his usual patrol around the yard he greeted her in a manner of unaccustomed friendliness.

"I hope I wasn't too short with you this morning, Miss Oliver," he said, with the energetic determination of a young man with sex on his mind. "About the ponytail, I mean."

The wide-eyed first grade teacher looked back at him with amazement, noticing that he was actually trying to smile at her, though the effort seemed a painful one.

"Oh, that's all right, Mr. Albrecht. I understand. No one likes getting hit in the eye. I should have held my ponytail while I was drinking at the fountain," she readily conceded, with a charming smile.

"Say, Miss Oliver, do you like the theatre?"

"The theater? Oh, I adore it."

"I have two tickets to West Side Story in Boston next week. Would you care to join me?"

"West Side Story?" she thrilled with excitement.

"Have you seen it?"

"No!"

"Will you come with me then?"

"Yes, thank you," she replied, after only a slight twinge of guilty hesitation.

"After all," thought Jessie, "Peter hasn't even kissed me yet. You can't really say we're going out. And Mr. Albrecht can apparently behave quite nicely when he wants." But then she remembered the way he treated the little boys and suddenly felt shocked at herself for accepting a date with him.

What would Peter think? Should she tell him? No, that would be awkward. But if she didn't tell him and he found out later, he would wonder why she had concealed it. Jessie decided to be perfectly honest with Peter and confess to him, right after the movies tonight. After all, she doubted that Peter could resist an invitation to see West Side Story himself, so he would surely understand.

Peter had never seen Jessie in a merrier mood. Once they entered the theatre it was all he could do to pull her away from the lobby cards for Frontier Gal. He noticed her staring at one in particular, the one with the spanking of Yvonne de Carlo. This publicity still seemed to mesmerize Jessie. Suddenly she turned to meet his eyes and blushed.

"That looks like a such thrilling scene," she explained, allowing herself to be lead away by the hand. Peter pondered this remark while House of Wax unfolded for them in 3-D. During the intermission they walked outside and Jessie smoked a cigarette. Peter bought her a lemonade and a paper of cotton candy for the next movie. The moon was up and dead leaves rattled through the windswept village street.

"This weather makes me tingle," she confessed.

"Something about the wind does stir the blood," Peter agreed, encouraged by the open expression of her animal spirits. Her obvious fascination with the spanking photograph was not lost on Peter, who was a highly intuitive man. He had wondered why she had been so eager to see a western from the 40's with no big stars. All week she could not hide her excitement at seeing this particular movie. Now he understood why. She was for some reason fixated on the spanking scene!

Jessie never removed her eyes from the screen during Frontier Gal and was rewarded with the unexpected spanking of the stubborn, six-year-old daughter by the handsome cowboy daddy halfway through the film.

"Wasn't that darling?" she whispered to Peter at the conclusion, wiping a tear from the corner of her eye with her handkerchief. Peter smiled at her and patted her tiny gloved hand.

"You're darling," he told her.

By the end of the film, watching her reactions and remembering certain snatches of conversations they had had, Peter was firmly convinced that Jessie had a spanking fetish. This pleased him no end, from both an erotic and a practical point of view. Faking an interest in the beat poets had him skating on thin ice, but when it came to a subject like spanking, he felt confident of delivering the goods. It was also heartening to realize that in spite of her liberated views, Jessie still entertained an old fashioned respect for the dominant male.

Peter took Jessie back to her apartment in a state of enchantment. When she invited him in for a bottle of wine, he did not demur but followed her immediately up to the third floor of the Victorian triple-decker house where she rented a sprawling apartment.

"Is a male visitor at this hour going to be a problem?"

"Goodness, no. My landlady is an artist with two lovers," Jessie replied, letting them in.

Peter lit a fire while she brought in the wine and glasses.

"Let me see that," he grabbed the bottle, read the label critically, then uncorked it and let it breathe.

"Is it okay?"

"Oh yes, excellent choice."

"You're just being polite."

"If it gets you tipsy, I'm satisfied," he candidly admitted.

"Oh, Peter, you certainly don't have to get me tipsy to take advantage of me. Not you of all people."

"Is that so?"

"Yes, but I have a confession to make."

"A confession?"

"Yes, Peter. I did something today of which I think you might disapprove and it's been troubling me."

"Oh?" Peter was mystified but very happy to learn that his approval mattered to Jessie. "Tell Peter, you'll feel ever so much better," he encouraged her.

So Jessie stammered out the news about her upcoming date in Boston with Mr. Albrecht. Peter had not seen this coming and felt momentarily shaken. Mr. Albrecht was younger, slicker, presumably more savvy, better dressed and earned more money than Peter. Moreover, Peter feared the vice principal's ruthless masculinity and cruel Richard Widmark lips would touch a cord in the latent masochist which would make her his slave in record time. Except for the fact that at this particular moment, he and he alone knew the secret to her heart.

"Peter?" she asked at length, "Aren't you going to say anything? Are you upset with me?"

"No, dear. Of course not," said Peter kindly. "It's not as though we have an understanding."

"But, we might have an understanding some day," she suggested, accepting a glass of wine.

"I'm sure you know that's entirely up to you, Jessie."

"Oh, I wish I hadn't said yes to that theatre date!" she declared, "But if I break it off now I'm sure he'll be offended."

"I suppose we don't want to offend Lionel," Peter reflected seriously.

"But I certainly don't want to offend you either!"

"Oh, don't worry about me," he reassured her. "I wouldn't think of rushing you into a commitment when we've only known each other six weeks."

"Oh, Peter, you're so understanding."

"Jessie, may I speak quite frankly without offending you?"

"Of course."

"For the sake of your reputation at school, soft peddle the free love stuff while you're out with Lionel."

"I will," she agreed thoughtfully, "or else he might think I'm easy and try something."

"Jessie, he'll try something in any case, but if you manage to look like the injured party rather than the - forgive me - sexy little piece that you are, you'll find it easier to control the situation in the long run."

"Do you really think I'm sexy, Peter?" Jessie glowed with pleasure and unconsciously wriggled in the tight, lacy one-piece foundation garment.

"I think you're naughty," he replied. Jessie blushed at this accusation, wondering where it would lead.

"Me? Oh no!" she demurred, her heart throbbing with anticipation.

"No? You don't think it's naughty to practically have an understanding with one man then make a date with another?"

"But, you said you weren't upset about that, Peter."

"I'm not upset, but I do think that we'd both feel much better if I were to give you a good spanking for making that date."

Jessie sat absolutely speechless while he took her wine glass away, removed his jacket and rolled his sleeves to the elbow. She had never felt such a blissful sensation in her life as the first moment he turned her over his knee. Peter had a comfortable lap and large hands, one of which curved around her small, corseted waist, to hold her firmly in place while the other rested dormant on the rise of her perky bottom. She could feel how large his hand was as he rested it on the seat of her skirt, almost covering it, for Jessie was rather slim hipped. He patted her lightly, sending thrills through her entire body with the touch of his hand.

Then he began to spank her, quickly and rhythmically, on either cheek, with a firm, sound stroke that caused a startled little "Oh!" to escape her lips the first few times his palm came down. The sounds she made thereafter were confined to pretty sighs and whimpers as the spanking progressed. Jessie had no desire to struggle away from her captor as the girls did in the movies. It felt too delicious to do anything but lie across his lap like a good little girl and take her spanking.

Peter had intended to stop after 20 or so swats, as they'd seen in the movie that evening, but when he saw how transported the spanking left Jessie, he carried on in the same style for a good twenty-five minutes, until he could feel the heat rising through her skirt. From the sounds she made and the way she wriggled and ground against him, Peter was certain that she was deriving many benefits from her spanking and felt deeply privileged to be the first one to bestow these upon the sweet girl.

Meanwhile, he himself was not unmoved. It felt exquisitely erotic to have the darling Jessie in this position, her tender sex pressed flat against his own burgeoning erection, through several discreet layers of clothes. He adored her bottom. And it was exhilarating to discover that he possessed the power to arouse her to such a degree. For never in the course of his (rather modest) love life, had he inspired such a vibrant response. He had always believed that spanking wasn't for children. Now he knew why.

"I think that's enough for now," he told her gently, finally pulling her up. She looked dazed and seemed to shudder when she looked at him. Then she smiled and put her arms around his neck.

"That's enough spanking for now," she corrected him, offering him her lips.

The next week was dreadfully confusing for Jessie. Friday night held her date with Lionel Albrecht in Boston and she couldn't help feeling guilty about not breaking it off in view of what had happened between her and Peter. But at the same time she had begun to wonder whether she could get Lionel to give her a spanking too. He seemed so naturally severe that the possibility did not seem nearly as remote as it had with pleasant, kindly Peter. But how to plant the suggestion in his head?

Jessie's parents lived in a large duplex apartment in Back Bay and it was to this residence she returned on nights when she attended the theatre in Boston. On this particular weekend, Jessie's parents were out of town, a fact that was not lost on Lionel as he asked to be invited in for a nightcap.

With a rapid pulse, Jessie offered him a brandy and sat down beside him on the loveseat facing the fire, which he had just lit. Possessing none of Peter's style or circumspection, within three minutes he was groping Jessie's firm, high bosom and running a hand up her leg.

"No!" Jessie said, pushing his hands away and moving away from him on the couch as much as possible.

"No?" he looked abashed. Lionel wasn't used to spending fifty dollars on a date and not getting something.

"Did you think I was that easy?" she pretended to be highly ruffled.

"I thought all Sarah Lawrence girls were broad-minded."

"Possibly, but not undiscriminating," she replied coolly.

"Hey, what's the matter with me?"

"First of all, you're rude. If attacking a girl is your idea of sophisticated seduction, you're sure to be rebuffed by any woman worth seducing," Jessie informed him.

"Humph," Lionel grunted, "you seem to know a lot about it. I assume you have been successfully seduced in the past?"

"You shouldn't assume any such thing, Mr. Albrecht!"

"No?" Lionel smiled at the idea of this quietly sophisticated young woman being a virgin.

"You might ask me what I consider to be permissible liberties," she temptingly suggested, emboldened by the several glasses of wine she'd consumed at the cafe after the theatre.

"Permissible liberties? Yes, do tell."

"Well, I will permit myself to be kissed, bitten lightly on the shoulders and– spanked."

"I'm sorry, did you say spanked?"

"Even a virgin can enjoy these innocent sensations, Mr. Albrecht."

"Call me Lionel," he said, removing his jacket and tie and taking her in his arms to kiss her. Jessie was amazed that he hadn't balked at her strange request and wondered as he kissed her and nibbled her ear lobes, whether he would remember to spank her as well.

Hot thrills exploded inside her as he lightly bit her shoulders, which were exposed by her sweetheart-cut cream velvet gown. Lionel, who was far from a brilliant conversationalist, did know how to handle women and soon had Jessie squirming.

In another instant he had pulled her across his lap and pushed her gown up to her waist. Jessie was astonished at the speed with which he had exposed her cream and pink ruffled panties, worn over a cream garter belt, which held up her sheer, nude tinted, seamed hose.

"So you're too discriminating to let me make love to you, are you?" Lionel brought his hand down hard on the exact center of her bottom. "And you say I'm rude!" Smack! His hand came down again, first on the right side, then on the left, then in the middle again.

"Remember, Jessie, you suggested this," he told her, hooking his fingers under her waist band and tugging her fancy briefs down to reveal her perfect, blushing bottom. "Now, spread your thighs," he ordered, pulling off her panties entirely, "you're getting a real spanking." And so saying he began to spank her very soundly, not neglecting to smack her tender thighs or hold her cheeks apart and spank her in between them as well, which drove her slightly mad with pleasure.

In a couple of minutes, Jessie became so wet with her own girlish essence that she began to smell deliriously provocative to Lionel. Spreading her labia gently with one hand he administered several light pats to her sex and brought his hand away wet.

"Explain yourself, young lady," he demanded, sticking his hand under her nose. "Or I'll have to punish you more severely," Lionel threatened, jumping into his new role as bedroom disciplinarian with shrewd alacrity. Lionel was not an epicure like Peter, but neither was he entirely crude and he could not fail to link Jessie's tangible excitement to the attentions he was paying her beautiful bottom. He had never been able to get a girl so wet so fast before. Not to mention the fact that the act of spanking her was more than enjoyable. He loved asserting himself over women.

"I'll teach you to flick me with your ponytail," he remembered with some satisfaction, as he brought his hand down vigorously on her already deeply reddened bottom. Meanwhile she was panting and squirming across his knee with every evidence of extreme pleasure. "Lie still," he ordered at length, "I need to examine you." Then she felt him pulling her open and inserting first one, then two fingers into her tingling sex. For a long time he held her down across his lap and alternated between masturbating and spanking her. Enraptured with this treatment, every thought of Peter fled and she gave herself up entirely to Lionel's stern, probing hands.

Finally, he unzipped his trousers, bent Jessie over the sofa arm and using her natural slickness to lubricate her anus, began to penetrate her bottom while firmly spreading her apart. Taking women in the bottom was Lionel's favorite way to have sex and he instinctively felt that if there was one woman who wouldn't protest this intimate intrusion, it was Jessie. After all, she had asked for a spanking.

Jessie was shocked and afraid when she felt his intention. She balked and pulled away.

"Jessie, this doesn't have to hurt. Just lie still and take what you've got coming like the bad little girl you are."

"It will hurt!" she insisted. "I can feel how big you are!"

"I know what I'm doing. Besides, once you relax you'll like it better than the other way."

"But I'm afraid!" she tried to pull away again. But Lionel had lost his patience with arguing and instead placed his hand in the small of her back and administered a dozen hard smacks to her up thrust backside.

"Now, are you going to cooperate or am I going to have to take off my belt?" he threatened, causing a fresh tremor to run through her.

"I'll cooperate," she squeaked, squirming with a mixture of acute embarrassment and unadulterated lust as he once again separated her cheeks and fed his engorged cock into her bottom.

"Relax!" he ordered, smacking her sharply on the thighs several times. Jessie took a deep breath but could barely let it out for excitement and fear, for she really was a virgin this way. But little by little, Lionel, who was a skillful sodomizer, changed that status, giving her the full length of his cock before very much longer and allowing her to flutter to an unexpected climax during the first few minutes of deep insertion.

Having done this much, he then felt more than justified in putting all his mighty thrusting power behind the twenty or so subsequent plunges necessary to spur his own exuberant orgasm.

"We weren't supposed to do that," she observed a few minutes later, while they were setting themselves to rights.

"I hope you're not sorry," he told her fervently, grabbing her hands and kissing them. "I don't think I've ever had a better time in my life."

"I never meant for it to go so far," she fretted, suddenly feeling horribly guilty about Peter.

"Well, what did you expect with an invitation like that?"

"Just some innocent thrills."

"And wasn't that exactly what we had?"

"Not really. You sodomized me."

"Was that the first time?"

"Yes!"

"I told you it wouldn't hurt."

"It did hurt a bit, at first. But then even the pain seemed exciting. And then the pain disappeared and it just felt very naughty. And then I came."

"And then I came. Isn't nature wonderful?"

"Now you won't respect me."

"Nonsense."

"You'll talk about me all over school."

"I'll do nothing of the sort."

"Now you think I'm cheap. Your kind always does."

"What do you mean my kind? Are you being fresh again? Because I still have some energy left to turn you over my knee one more time."

"But, did you enjoy it too?" she blurted out, flushing all over at the new threat.

"I'm telling you quite honestly that it was the best."

"You were rather abrupt," she critically observed. "Why, you didn't even give me the opportunity to decline the sex. You slapped me harder when I tried to!"

"You didn't really mind, did you?"

"I suppose I didn't, really. But I hope you don't act that way with every girl you go out with!"

"Every girl I go out with doesn't ask for a spanking."

"Oh, I'm sure that had nothing to do with your actions," Jessie perceived. "After all, you were groping me before I discussed permissible liberties."

"What are you saying?"

"With all due respect, you practically raped me."

"Oh, nonsense. You were wetter than any girl I've ever seen in my life."

"That's not the point."

"I think it is."

"Perhaps I'm just perverse enough to respond to your rough attentions, in spite of myself. But I daresay your approach would scare the living daylights out of most girls."

"I understand what's happening here," said Lionel, who had been a psychology major at NYU. "You feel guilty because you had a climax, so now you're trying to pin all the responsibility on me."

"Is that what I'm doing?"

"Obviously."

"I'll have to ponder that."

"Do. Meanwhile, I'll say good night."

Jessie walked him to the door and let him kiss her, wanting very much to tell him the real reason for her unease. But still not knowing Lionel's true character, she hesitated to introduce Peter as a rival. Her growing feeling for Peter made protecting the gentle teacher an imperative.

"Good night, Lionel," she said.

"Will we see each other again?" he asked.

"I don't think so," she replied steadily. This reply was not the one he wanted or expected and his lips compressed into a thin line.

"Okay, fine. Just keep kidding yourself you're a good girl," he snapped and strode out into the corridor to punch the elevator button. Jessie closed the door behind him feeling as though she'd behaved as badly as she could have that night, both to Peter and Lionel.

Jessie spent the weekend in torment, not knowing what to tell Peter when he asked her about her date. She still hadn't decided on a story when rainy Monday morning arrived. Mercifully, lunchroom duty made Jessie unavailable for their usual bench date. However, Peter made a point of stopping by the lunchroom and handing her a little brown bag with a sandwich and cupcake. Jessie almost cried, feeling more guilty than ever. Noticing her stricken look, Peter instantly apprehended much of what had passed between Lionel and Jessie and felt quite awkward as he made a hasty retreat from the lunchroom.

It seemed a perfect eternity to the three o'clock bell and Jessie's nerves were in tatters by the time it rang. Now there were raincoats to be buttoned and galoshes to pull on, all of which took another ten minutes. Finally she was able to usher the double line of sturdy little six-year-olds into the yard to be claimed by their parents, big brothers and sisters or the school bus. By three-thirty the yard was clear. Jessie unfurled her beige umbrella and began to walk home through the village, picking her way through the puddles in her high heels wrapped in dainty, clear plastic button-up over-boots. On the way she stopped at the tearoom and cheered herself with a pot of tea and a dish of French pastries.

"Hi, Jessie, mind if I join you?"

Jessie looked up at Miss Kranz, who was very chic in a belted, black raincoat and matching cloche over her short-cropped, light red hair.

"Not at all, Lorna," Jessie declared, welcoming the distraction from her worrying.

"They say it's going to rain for the next week," Lorna Kranz informed her fellow instructor.

"M'm," Jessie wondered if the strict third grade teacher was going to say anything interesting to her. Then, all at once, she did.

"How did you like West Side Story?" Lorna slyly asked.

"Pardon me?"

"I saw you at the performance the other night. With Lionel Albrecht."

"Oh! Well, it was just wonderful. Wasn't it?"

"Magnificent."

"Yes."

"So, are you seeing Lionel?"

"No. Decidedly not!" Jessie replied vehemently. Then she took a second look at the impeccable twenty-five year-old across the table. "Why? Do you like him?"

"Well, to tell you the truth, I never thought of him as being available until I saw him with you."

"That's funny. He never thought of me as being available until he saw me with Mr. Johanson. But the truth is, Mr. Johanson is the one I have the crush on."

"How interesting."

"Perhaps if Lionel knew that you were interested in him he'd ask you out."

"But you're not interested in Lionel yourself?"

"Not really. I like Mr. Johanson," Jessie said fervently. Lorna actually smiled. As with Lionel, the act seemed both painful and difficult. "You'd be much better suited to Lionel than me," Jessie suggested.

"Really? Why do you say so?"

"Well, with all due respect, you're both so strict."

"Strict?" Lorna didn't understand.

"With the children."

"Oh!" the third grade teacher again tried to smile.

"Why are you so strict with the children?"

"Because it's the only way to make them pay attention. You don't know that because your little first graders are docile and frightened of their own shadow. But third graders can be extremely rambunctious."

"I see," Jessie nodded, wondering if she hadn't misjudged Miss Kranz.

"As for Lionel, he has to be tough. Remember, he's dealing with boys as old as old as ten and eleven. Would you rather they ran wild and turned into delinquents?"

"No," said Jessie meekly.

"Discipline is crucial to education."

"I suppose that's true."

"So you really think that Lionel and I would be compatible?"

"Oh, I'm convinced of it. Now that I think of it, I'm sure I've seen him covertly admire your beautiful figure before."

"You're sweet," said Lorna, putting some change down on the table for a tip. "I've got to run, honey. But thanks for the chat."

"It's all confidential, though," Jessie warned.

"I understand," Lorna actually gave her a wink as she breezed out of the tearoom and into the rain swept street.

Now Jessie was able to continue home with a spring in her step. Lorna Kranz liked Lionel Albrecht. She now knew he was available. She was not the type of woman the average mere male (which Lionel certainly was) could resist. Not with legs and a waist like that and a closet full of designer copies. News like this might possibly mitigate Peter's disappointment at her behavior once she made her awful confession to him.

Generally Jessie did her errands and chores between four and six, dined simply and worked on her lesson plan for the following day directly after dinner. But today she was so distracted she knew if she didn't do her lesson plan first, it might never get done. So the moment she got home, she made herself a pot of coffee and arranged her textbooks upon her kitchen table. By five thirty she had finished her work and leaned back in her chair to enjoy a cigarette. Then she reached for the phone and dialed Peter's number.

"Hello?" he answered on the first ring.

"Peter, it's Jessie. What are you doing?"

"Just peeling potatoes for dinner."

"I didn't have a chance to get to the market today, myself."

"Why don't you come over? You know I love feeding you."

"May I?"

"Please do, but drive carefully. It's raining pretty hard."

"I will!"

In less than fifteen minutes she was at Peter's cottage door, clutching a bottle of her father's best burgundy, which she'd pilfered over the weekend. Peter studied the label and smiled.

"Thank you!"

"What are you cooking?"

"Roast beef."

"Mmmm! I picked the right night to invite myself for dinner."

"You know you're always welcome. In fact, I wish you'd never leave," he declared, then went out to the kitchen with the wine to hide his embarrassment. She hung her raincoat in the closet and followed him out to the kitchen, where she sat down on a wooden settle and asked him to help her remove her outer boots.

"With pleasure," he told her, unbuttoning each one and yanking it off with the efficiency of a man who'd been tugging galoshes on and off children's tiny feet for fifteen years.

"Oh, Peter!" she sighed, throwing her arms around his neck and hugging him hard. This gesture made it fairly clear to Peter that whatever had happened between Jessie and Lionel, it hadn't won her away from him yet. In fact, she looked as happy to be in his house as he felt to have her there.

"All right, young lady, come clean. What happened this weekend in Boston between you and Lionel?"

The question popped out so abruptly that for a moment she could only stare at him with wide eyes. Then she dropped her gaze and looked ashamed.

"I'm afraid I didn't behave very well in Boston, Peter," she admitted, watching him pop the sliced potatoes into boiling water.

"Oh dear."

"I did everything wrong thing I could possibly do!" she confessed passionately.

"I guessed as much when I saw you at lunch today."

"You're going to be disappointed in me," she told him with conviction.

"Only if you tell me that you've fallen in love with that brute."

"Oh no! I could never love a man of so little finesse! Not to mention his harshness with the children."

"Then I'm not losing my girl to Lionel?"

"Oh never, Peter!" She went to him and wrapped her arms around his waist from behind to press the whole length of her torso against his straight back.

"Please, Jessie, not while I'm slicing an onion," he scolded, his eyes watering profusely. She released him and retired to a kitchen stool.

"So you're not upset?"

"Why should I be upset?"

"Because of what I did."

"Well, Jessie, I'm not sure I understand exactly what you did do." He deftly carved radish rosettes.

"I allowed Lionel to sodomize me."

Peter stared at her in surprise. "You did what?"

"I pretended to be a good girl, as you suggested, but got greedy for sensations and told Lionel that he might spank me. He interpreted that as an invitation to take my bottom, thus satisfying his need to humiliate me while preserving my alleged virginity."

"You told Lionel about the spanking thing?" Peter was more shocked by this than the idea of Lionel inserting his undeserving penis into Jessie's divine bottom.

"I offered it as a substitute for sex."

"But you wound up having sex anyway."

"He virtually forced himself on me, Peter. Though once I'd become visibly aroused from the spanking, my protests had a hollow ring. He's a sexual predator, just as you suspected and I was easy game."

"Well, how was it?" Peter asked stiffly, for some reason feeling more piqued at the other man for spanking Jessie than violating her.

"You mean the spanking? Well, as you might expect from Lionel, it was rather too hard. All the same, I knew he was only thinking of sex and not of correcting me at all."

"But you said you became aroused," said Peter, shucking corn and dropping it into boiling water.

"Well, of course I did. I get aroused when Little Nancy in the comics gets a spanking, so of course when a handsome man does it –"

"Lionel does cut a dashing figure, I suppose," Peter granted gloomily.

"But I find you a hundred times more attractive, Peter," Jessie confided.

"Still, Jessie, I thought you shared your special secret with me because you liked me and knew you could trust me. Now here I find you've told it to a man you neither like nor find trustworthy!"

"As I said, Peter, I was recklessly curious."

"And look what happened! Lionel took advantage of you." Peter found himself actually becoming angry with Jessie.

"He certainly did."

"You know, if you'd behaved like the good girl you were pretending to be and said goodnight on the stoop, none of this would have happened." Peter declared with a degree of irritation that set Jessie's tummy fluttering.

"I intended to be good."

Peter checked the kitchen clock and saw that he had about ten minutes before the corn had to come out of the water. He therefore purposefully removed his apron, pulled a heavy oaken chair into the center of the floor, sat down on it and patted his thigh. "Come over here, young lady."

Jessie gingerly approached him and within an instant of coming into grabbing reach, found herself thrust face down across his sturdy lap.

"I can't believe you allowed that reprehensible bully so many liberties," he sternly declared, bringing his hand down hard on her skirted bottom.

"I'm very sorry," she gasped, startled by the vigor of his first few smacks.

"You had no business accepting that date in the first place," said Peter in a way that filled Jessie with secret contentment.

"You should have insisted I break it!" she asserted, casting him a look at him over one shoulder.

"Oh? It's my fault, is it?" Smack! Smack! Smack!

"You should have forbidden me to go!" she interjected at the first pause.

"I might have if I'd known that you were going to behave like a little tart."

"Oh!" she cried, twisting on his lap to avoid the next swat, "how dare you call me that?"

"It's the mildest word I can think of for a girl who acts like you," he informed her, locking her hand to her side and continuing to spank her soundly.

"To apply that word to me is quite unfair," she interrupted him haughtily.

"Oh? How so?" he paused to rub the sting away for a moment.

"Because it implies immorality and neither of us believe that sex outside of wedlock is immoral!"

"What it implies is disloyalty, and you know quite well that you're guilty of that!"

Jessie pondered this accusation as the spanking continued.

"You let another man possess you when you know you love me!" Peter declared with sudden confidence.

"Yes. That is true," she softly agreed, gladdening his heart. He stopped, let her up, took her back on his lap the right way around and embraced her. "Is my spanking over?" she shyly inquired.

"For as naughty as you've been? By no means. But I have to tend the stove for a few seconds now," Peter said, putting her off his lap. She rubbed her bottom through her dress while she watched him turn off the heat under the corn, turn it down under the potatoes and baste the roast. Then he turned to her. "We've got about a half hour until it's all ready. Shall we go upstairs?"

A winding wooden staircase led to a bedroom loft. "Sit down," he told her, motioning to the wide upholstered bench at the foot of his large maple four-poster bed. She obeyed in quiet excitement

"Now, Jessie," he began, leaning against the wooden wardrobe opposite with folded arms, "in view of your recent admission that you love me–"

"Did I say that?"

"You didn't disagree when I said it."

"Oh, that's right," she smiled at him.

"As I was saying, in view of the fact that you love me, your behavior over the weekend with Lionel seems all the more inexcusable."

Jessie hung her head.

"Jessie, like you, I believe in the validity of free love, but what happened between you and Lionel does not fall under that classification."

"It doesn't?"

"No, you simply allowed a man you don't like to pressure you into sex. No love entered into the equation as far as I can see."

"Except for my love of spanking and Lionel's love of sex."

Peter was momentarily taken aback and realized with excitement that he had finally met a girl who could think.

"Nevertheless," he replied firmly, "if we're going to be lovers, you can't see other men."

"I won't!" she promised fervently.

"I tried treating you like an adult, trusting you to go out with Lionel and behave yourself, and look what happened. Now you say I should have forbidden you to go. Does that mean you need to be restricted like a child? Threatened with corporal punishment at the first hint of mischief?"

"Oh, yes, please!" Jessie cried. Peter picked up a hairbrush, tossed it in the air and caught it. She followed its path like a cat enthralled with a bird.

"Now, Jessie, if you really are the good girl you pretend to be, you won't feel easy until you've been properly punished for your crimes against our love, isn't that so?"

"Yes, sir," she said in a soft voice that thrilled him.

"In fact, you've been so naughty that a simple spanking will not be enough."

"What else then?" she grew wide-eyed with curiosity, wondering whether he would take off his belt.

"Have you ever been given an enema?"

"No," she slowly replied, her face reddening instantly.

"Oh, it's quite a popular punishment for naughty little girls."

"I wasn't punished much as a child."

"Well, we can make up for that now."

"But why would you –" she faltered for words, "– do that sort of thing to me?"

"Well, for one thing, I think it would help you pay better attention to your spanking."

"But I would do that in any case!"

"Jessie, I'm not going to argue with you. Take your dress off and hang it in the closet right now."

Jessie had on a white silk full slip under her dress and a matching combination of bra, garter belt and panties under that. She shyly hung up her dress and turned to look at him.

Peter took a couple of pillows out of a linen chest and piled them one on top of the other in the center of the bed.

"I want you face down with the pillows under your tummy," he ordered. She slowly assumed this position. "No, dear, don't lean up on your elbows, lie down." When Jessie obeyed him he sat beside her on the bed and slowly arranged her exactly the way he wanted her for the delicate operation to follow. "Perhaps you'd better close your eyes and just let this happen," he told her, pulling up her slip, and lowering her lace trimmed briefs to mid-thigh. Her bottom was as white and pink as a hybrid rose from the spanking and her sex gave off as heady a scent.

"I'm going to leave you for three minutes and you are going to lie quite still until I return. Do you understand me, young lady?"

"Yes," she meekly replied, squirming with embarrassment over the pillows, though she knew she must look very attractive with her new panties and garter belt from Paris framing her smooth bottom.

Peter disappeared into the adjoining bathroom for the promised three minutes, returning with a pile of towels and a jar of petroleum jelly, which he set on the bed.

"Close your eyes," he told her, which she did the moment she glimpsed the very full hot water bag which he somehow contrived to suspend from one of the posts of the bed. "Lift up, darling," he said gently, tucking several towels under her tummy before pressing her back down on the pillows. "Now just lie still and let me examine you," said Peter, choosing one of Jessie's favorite words.

Now she felt him spreading her bottom and lubricating her deeply with two fingers.

"I hope you realize, Jessie, that you brought this humiliation on yourself," Peter told her, spreading her for the nozzle now and gently inserting it between her cheeks. "You wanted to sample new sensations? Well, you're about to feel a very interesting one."

"I already am!" she murmured, squirming around the nozzle as he plunged it four inches into her bottom.

"Now hold perfectly still," he warned her, and holding her in place with one hand on her bottom, he released the clamp on the hose and allowed the flow of water to begin.

"Oh!" she cried breathlessly as she began to feel the warm water fill her. "Are you sure it won't come out?" she asked fearfully.

"You just lie still and behave, I'll take care of everything else," he told her, lifting her by the hips and adjusting her a little higher over the pillows. Then he pulled her panties off entirely, separated her legs and encouraged her to bend her knees slightly, elevating her bottom yet a little higher. "Now you can lean on your elbows a bit," he told her, moving her into more of a modified all fours position, with her bottom uppermost. "Good girl," he told her, slipping one hand under her satiny stomach to feel it slowly expand as the water filled her. Jessie gave a little moan of embarrassed excitement as he gently squeezed her abdomen and patted her bottom.

"Jessie, dear?"

"Yes, Peter?"

"This may feel a little bit uncomfortable, but it isn't supposed to hurt, so tell me if it does."

"I will."

Peter shut the clamp several times during the two-quart infusion to let her adjust to the sensation of so much warm water filling her. Jessie became very wet and wondered why he considered this a punishment. Except for the embarrassment, which was substantial indeed, these attentions felt as ticklishly sexy as the anal sex with Lionel, but with none of the pain of forced cramming.

Finally the hot water bottle was empty and Jessie was very full. But still she felt no discomfort, or at least, very little. In a moment he had removed the nozzle and pressed her down on the pillows again. "Don't move," he told her, unhooking the enema apparatus from the bedpost and disappearing into the bathroom for a moment.

He returned with a few more thick towels, which he draped across his lap when he sat down on the bed. Then he very carefully pulled her across his lap as well. "But I'm afraid I'll have an accident!" she cried. "I'm so full."

"You'd better not have an accident," he warned her sternly, then calmly picked up his hairbrush.

Since it was a heavy, wooden, square, men's brush, he only had to tap her with it to leave a bright pink imprint on her pearly flesh. Even so, each slow and measured stroke made her sting and smart. And yet being in this position, with her tummy so full and her whole sex aching with excitement, the pain was somehow merged into rhapsodic pleasure and she could not bring herself to protest, even when the strokes grew more severe.

Jessie had always wanted to take a hard spanking. But she had also feared it. Now, with her senses all aflame through his attentions to her bottom, her mind was open to the discipline. She felt each stroke go through her now and heard herself whimper as they fell, but still she wanted more. She really did want to feel punished, but only by Peter, because she was so certain of his ardent admiration and love.

And then, all at once, she reached her crisis and spasmed violently across his lap, gasping with the delirious sensation of coming from a spanking. He put the brush down and stroked her gently until her tremors subsided and she gingerly slipped off his lap. He pointed in the direction of the bathroom and left her to scamper through the door while he went back downstairs to put dinner on the table.

Lionel knew he had made a negative impression on Jessie, which he attempted to soften by sending her flowers. She didn't have an opportunity to thank him until the following afternoon when she had just dismissed her class in the schoolyard. It was another stormy day and she was headed towards the village haberdashery to order a Donegal tweed jacket for Peter to arrive by Christmas. Meanwhile, Peter had strolled off to the village jewelers to purchase an engagement ring. For although Jessie had said she did not care to be married, she'd made no prohibition against being engaged.

Lionel fell into step with Jessie, surprising her into a gasp.

"It's only me."

"Oh, Lionel. Hello," Jessie smiled cordially.

"Still mad at me?"

"I was never mad at you, Lionel. And thank you for the beautiful flowers."

"You said I practically raped you," he brooded, for he hadn't quite been able to get that accusation out of his mind all weekend, particularly the idea of her telling people that.

"You did, but I suppose I don't blame you. After all, I was very provocative."

"Yes, you were. Listen; explain this spanking thing to me. You seemed to like it."

"You seemed to like it too," Jessie observed, wondering whether she ought to change the subject at once, since it was beginning to make her blush and throb all over. She couldn't look at Lionel's chiseled profile without remembering that just a few short days before he'd actually taken her across his knee and paddled her quite effectively, not to mention penetrating her most secret place and giving her a very real climax in the process. There was a limit to how unfriendly Jessie could feel towards a man of such abilities, but the memory of Peter's masterful lovemaking so fresh in her mind confused her emotions.

"Do other women like it the way you do? I mean, is this a regular practice, taking a spanking instead of having sex?"

Jessie laughed, "I don't know, but I'll bet it would be fun to try the experiment with Miss Kranz."

"Lorna? That frigid bundle of nerves?"

"Lionel!" Jessie was shocked. "And she spoke so well of you!"

"Well of me? In what context?"

"I believe she admires you greatly both as a man and an educational administrator," Jessie revealed.

"Really?" Lionel smiled slightly.

"Don't you think she's got the most ravishing figure? And those legs."

Lionel looked at Jessie sharply. "So I'm getting the brush off, am I?"

"I'm sorry," she lowered her eyes as they splashed through the cobblestone puddles.

"Was it the way I acted?"

"No, Lionel. I just don't feel we're temperamentally suited."

After they parted at the door of the haberdashery, Lionel walked back to his car thinking about Lorna Kranz.

Over the next couple of days, Lionel and Lorna began to look each other in the eyes for the first time, though hers were always the first to be lowered. And although he preferred Jessie's rounder contours and rosy face, Lionel certainly admired the appearance of the meticulously groomed and gracefully slender redhead. Her ivory skin was without blemish and he'd never seen such an elegant instep. Lorna always wore the highest heels, which gave her taut, little bottom an additional lift.

"Now there's a girl who really needs a spanking," thought Lionel of the fussy and exacting third grade teacher, who seemed the type who would hold out for a wedding ring in the face of any sexual temptation, which was why he had never bothered to pursue her. But Jessie had said that Lorna liked him and this single piece of data took him half the way to liking her.

However, Lionel had no patience with virgins. He had a strong sex drive which he enjoyed exercising and switched partners often. So far he had mostly avoided emotional involvements. Since he was a jagged, driven and not at all comforting male, there had never been much inducement for a girlfriend to want to capture and domesticate him. Women sensed that he was a critical, inflexible man and shied away from him after a couple of dates, in spite of the rather satisfying sex.

He hadn't gone out with a good girl since high school and wondered whether it was worth the bother. In the end he decided to wait until Lorna made the first move. She did it rather gracefully during a faculty meeting, when Lionel called for a volunteer to head the decorations committee for the Christmas Pageant. This meant several meetings alone in his office for funds to be dispensed and receipts collected.

Lorna had been an art major at Boston University and welcomed the opportunity to show off a few of her skills. Lionel noticed that each time she was due to appear in his office she went to great pains to wear a smart new outfit and her highest heels.

During the week of the pageant she acquitted herself admirably, turning the school auditorium into Santa's Workshop. Jessie's class contributed some of the snowflakes. And of course, Peter played holiday songs while the children sang.

"You did an excellent job on the decorations, Lorna," Lionel complimented her that afternoon after all of the children had departed for the Christmas holidays. "Will you let me buy you an eggnog at the Inn to celebrate your brilliant achievement?" he asked courteously, which thrilled her to the core.

"Thank you, Lionel," she agreed at once and they walked down the cold, windswept streets of Random Point towards the ancient Bone and Feather Inn.

Two eggnogs later, Lorna was giggling in a red leather booth with Lionel.

"How do you plan to spend the holidays?" he asked her casually.

"I'm going to spend the whole time painting," she confided.

"Oh really? What kind of painting do you do?"

"I paint in various styles. Right now I'm in my abstract impressionist phase."

"That's interesting," he said with surprise, for the last thing he expected Lorna to say was something interesting about herself. "I'd like to see your work."

"Follow me home in your car and I'll show you some of it," she suggested. Lionel almost smiled. This was going better than he expected.

"Where do you live?" he asked as they left the pub and emerged into the rain again.

"I have a studio in the old lighthouse," she told him, unfurling her black umbrella as they walked back to their cars. Now Lionel was really intrigued. He'd imagined that Lorna lived with her parents.

Lorna's studio above the pounding surf seemed to Lionel the perfect setting for a seduction. When they arrived she gave him a brandy then went into her bedroom to change into a pair of black Capri pants, a cream silk tunic and black leather flats. Her autumnal colored page boy was perfectly silky and straight, the sort of hair that women never worried about disarranging because it always fell right back into place. She really was a striking young lady, he reflected when she sat

33

down beside him on the divan.

"Well? Do you like any of them?" Lorna gestured around the room to the many oils, watercolors, charcoals, crayon sketches and cartoons that lined the richly painted walls of her studio.

"You're very accomplished," he remarked truthfully, his respect deepening for Lorna as he realized that she was anything but ordinary.

"Thank you."

Lionel waited until she finished her tumbler of brandy before making his move, which was to take her in his arms and kiss her. Lorna was powerfully attracted to Lionel and had been since the first day they met, the year before. But unlike Jessie, Lorna was cool-headed and quite able to marshal her passions when her common sense sounded an alarm. This was exactly what happened when Lionel began to unbutton her tunic in order to fondle her small and perfectly formed bosom.

"I'm sorry," she said firmly, pushing his hand away and escaping from his embrace, "but there's only so far I'm willing to go on a first date."

"Here we go," thought Lionel with a sigh. And her artistic sensibilities had given him such high hopes the moment before.

"Okay, I'll say good night then," he replied shortly, getting to his feet.

"But, I didn't mean for you to leave," she suddenly said, perversely inflamed by his coldness.

"No?" He sat back down.

"Cigarette?" she offered him one and he accepted. She lit his then her own and regarded him thoughtfully before speaking again. "Don't be sullen just because you can't get your lust-engorged member wet tonight," she suddenly shocked him by saying. "Instead you ought to remember the adage, 'All good things come to those who wait.'"

"How long do I have to wait?" he demanded, looking at her with increased respect.

"I'll let you know when I decide."

Lionel didn't know now whether to go or stay. Normally a situation like this would frustrate him so badly that all he would want to do was get away from the offending female. But somehow, sex or no sex, he didn't quite feel like leaving Lorna yet.

"I'll take another brandy while you're thinking it over," he told her, handing her his empty glass. As she walked past him toward the pantry he deliberately smacked her on the bottom. Lorna gasped and turned to look at him with a vivid blush, which he duly noted. She refilled his glass and took a long pull on hers as she came to sit beside him again.

Was it an illusion, Lionel wondered, or did that one, sharp smack do something to Lorna? She'd become very quiet and wide-eyed all at once.

"You know, giving you a good, sound spanking would be as satisfying as anything to me," Lionel proposed, surprising himself as much as Lorna. But the truth was that ever since the week before with Jessie, the thrill of spanking had lingered in his mind, blending in quite comfortably with his aggressive notions about sex.

"A spanking?" She did not sound affronted in the slightest. "You mean, over your knee?"

"That's right, over my knee. For being a little tease."

"I am not a tease!"

"You wore four-inch heels to school today, Lorna. Because you wanted every male in the building to follow those long legs wherever you went."

"I simply like to dress smartly," she said, still blushing furiously at the promised trip across Lionel's knee.

"Who do you think you're kidding?" Lionel took her gently by the forearm and pulled her across his lap, astonished that she didn't resist.

Lorna wondered whether Lionel had also spanked Jessie and that was the reason the pretty blonde teacher had evinced such a dislike for him. Lorna had never had a man offer to spank her before, but she found she didn't mind the idea. She had always thrilled to spankings in the movies when the disciplinarian was a handsome leading man. Lionel was certainly handsome. His profession was that of a disciplinarian. And although a petty tyrant herself, she respected his authority as her superior. Perhaps it was partially the fault of the alcohol, but Lorna felt a perfect explosion of butterflies in her flat, little tummy as he pulled her across his lap and locked his arm around her waist.

"Is this what you did to Jessie when she withheld her favors?" she boldly inquired before the first smack fell. Lionel pushed her tunic up to her waist while he decided how to reply. His ego urged him to reveal that Jessie's favors had not been withheld. He also wondered whether such a revelation might spur Lorna to give in as well, so as not to be deemed less sophisticated than a child like Jessie. But in the end honor dictated the only possible answer.

"Oh, my date with Jessie was strictly platonic."

"Oh, I see."

"And besides," Smack! "She's not a little flirt!" Smack! "She doesn't wear jersey dresses that outline her bottom like a glove." Smack! Smack!

"I wasn't aware of a dress code for teachers," she replied, wriggling across his lap under the first few smacks.

"You dress beautifully, darling. I wouldn't change a thing about it. The only problem is, it makes men think about sex."

A sound spanking followed, giving Lorna plenty of time to decide whether she liked it. Lorna took every stroke without protest, though towards the end of the count of one hundred, she'd begun to breathe rather heavily. She couldn't account for it, but the spanking felt distinctly pleasurable. She was aware of a sting and later of a tangible heat rising from her skin and penetrating through the silk trousers, but the sensations she was receiving could not be termed painful. Pain was hitting one's head on a kitchen cabinet. This sensation was purely erotic.

To Lionel's great joy, Lorna's trousers were zipped in back. He had been gratified to the point of a raging erection by the way she had taken her spanking so far and had little reason to doubt she would allow him to pull her pants down. Therefore he unzipped them courageously, waited for her to protest, and when she did not, briskly pulled them down to reveal the sheerest black nylon panties he had ever seen. As in a Vargas illustration, her white skin glowed through the filmy material, highlighted by areas of dark pink.

Now he began all over again on her slim, elegant, oval-cheeked pantied bottom. The pants came off in a minute, revealing her slender legs and Lionel congratulated himself on getting her half undressed without the slightest protest. Amazingly, he'd met the second girl in two weeks who seemed to enjoy discipline.

While he was warming her panties, Lionel thought back to the times when he had impulsively pulled an ex-girlfriend over his knee. The response had never been what he was getting now, so he had eventually stopped doing it. But now that he'd met Jessie and Lorna, he realized that he was deriving a certain indefinable pleasure from domination. Lionel knew he was skillful in extracting sex from women, which was a compulsion in itself. But this felt satisfying on a different level.

Lorna became very responsive. Soon she began to arch to his hand and slightly spread her legs. Lionel smiled, pressing his fingers between her smooth, white thighs and feeling how damp her panties had become. She spread her thighs a little wider, encouraging him ever so slightly to touch her there once more. He still held her firmly around the waist while he stroked and probed her lightly through her panties. Lorna had begun to whimper, quite overwhelmed by the feeling of all these curious attentions and aching to have her panties pulled down.

"I'm not through with you yet," he told her, slowly pulling her beautiful panties down to expose her glowing cheeks. She did not try to stop him and once they were down, allowed him to caress her warm, bare skin. Now he began to spank her slowly and significantly, making each swat count. She waited patiently, and then caught her breath each time his hand came down.

Now and then he would pause to lightly stroke her between her legs with deft fingertips. She was now sopping wet and unequivocally receptive. Soon he drove her frantic by not quite fingering her slippery sex between smacks. He did, however, spread her open, mercilessly exposing all of her tender, inner charms to his own devouring gaze. This was another good tease and Lorna's practically unused little clitoris throbbed painfully, begging for firmer attentions.

It was at this poignant juncture that Lionel decided, quite uncharacteristically, not to complete the conquest, either by spanking her to a climax or possessing her then and there, both of which were entirely within his grasp. Instead, for once he mastered his own insistent desire long enough to decide that he had finally found a girl worth fascinating. He instinctively sensed that the only way to do this was to appear stronger and more disciplined than she was. The crack she had made earlier about him being so eager to get his penis wet still stung him as the sort of rebuke a sophisticated woman deals a teenaged boy smitten with her. He was now determined to make her beg for sex before he gave it to her.

At length he let her up and looked very serious as he said, "That should give you something to remember me by tonight."

Lorna was still gasping from the hard but very erotic spanking she had just received and looked at him respectfully.

"I'll say good night now," he told her, "but I'll call you tomorrow, if I may."

"Yes, Lionel," she said, rubbing her bottom gingerly and looking at him in some surprise. Was he really leaving? Now that she was more warmed up than she had ever been? Lorna scrambled back into her pants to see him out, wondering whether she should say something about her condition.

"Are you going to be a good girl until I see you again?" he asked, taking her in his arms in the stone stairwell with the moon lit portal window. He kissed her firmly several times, gave her a long hug, a good squeeze and a final pat on the bottom before going out the door into the brisk night air. Lorna sat in the stone stairwell for some time, thinking about what had happened.

Lionel went home to his old stone house on the outskirts of the village and masturbated to the memory of Lorna's beauty and grace as she lay across his lap with her bottom reddening under his relentless hand. After that he felt more relaxed than he had in years.

"How's my little prude today?" Lionel pleasantly asked Lorna, slipping into a booth opposite her at the China Star restaurant during the Monday afternoon lunch break. He had seen her walk into the village and followed her there. She flushed as he sat down but smiled a little too.

"I'm not a prude and you know it," she returned, steadily pouring him a tiny cup of tea.

"When can I see you again?" he asked.

"Did you have such a good time?"

"I had a very good time!" he declared. "You know how I'm usually all wound up?" Lorna nodded. "Not since I gave you that spanking."

"Do tell, Lionel," Lorna was amused.

"It released a lot of tension."

"I'm glad I could be so helpful."

"Would you mind having a husband who spanked you regularly?" Lionel astonished himself as well as Lorna by asking.

"Since I intend to be the perfect wife, I can't imagine that gentleman finding reasons to spank me regularly," Lorna declared, glowing with pleasure at the welcome proposal.

"Really? Do you intend to stop wearing tight skirts and high heels after you're married?"

"Certainly not!"

"Then there will always be reasons to spank you regularly, my dear."

Chapter Two

Anthony and Paige

Anthony Newton did not expect to form attachments to two new women that winter. In response to Susan's unfaithfulness, he had thought of adding one girl at most. However, the changes began without planning, when his secretary of many years decided to retire and he asked her to name her replacement.

"She must be unobtrusive, Agnes," he stipulated. "No one too high powered or exhaustingly ambitious. And no cupcakes."

Mrs. O'Connor smiled. "I think I may be able to recommend someone you'll like. A niece of mine named Paige. She's currently working in Customer Service at Macy's."

"Good. That requires tact. How old is she?"

"31."

"Oh. I was hoping she'd be older. Is she married?"

"No."

"That's not good. However, it may work out so long as she's modest and plain."

"Paige isn't glamorous, but I think you'll find her pleasant and agreeable."

"Have her come in today."

Later that day, Anthony watched from his study window as an awkward girl walked up the street to his brownstone. He noted her trim figure in her beige trench coat as she fumbled with her umbrella and frowned at his secretary. "She doesn't look all that plain to me, Agnes. And are you sure you said 31? She looks 23."

A few minutes later, as Anthony shook Paige's slim unmanicured hand, he noticed with a feeling of uneasiness, her creamy pink complexion fringed with freckles, complimenting to perfection her blue eyes. She was of medium height, with straight, shoulder length brown hair, pulled back in a metal barrette, with neither bangs nor earrings to offset the severity of her flat hair do. Her knit polyester suit was electric blue with black piping and did not become her. His practiced eye replaced all of these discordant externals with a geometric haircut, tailored clothes, expensive shoes and dark lipstick. Her features were regular and her proportions good. Anthony saw in her rosy face the elusive Catholic high school girl of his youth who had served as the focus of a hundred fantasies.

Even the heavy Bronx accent could be eradicated in time, he mused, as he fretted about whether to hire her. When she shyly confided how much she loved his music and he saw how tenderly respectful she was, Anthony heard alarms. He would inevitably start to dress her, she would suddenly look adorable and then he would inevitably begin to undress her.

Paige was university educated. He noticed that she thought before she spoke and did not utter irrelevant remarks. Her demeanor was naturally one of alert compliance. He knew as he beheld her honest, innocent face, that she would make a splendid assistant.

"All right, Agnes, we'll give Paige a chance," he told her aunt when she had gone. "But I can't believe she works at Macy's and dresses like that. Get her some clothes before she starts."

Mrs. O'Connor's wardrobe choices for her niece weren't elegant, but she did stay on for two weeks, training Paige. Then, at the beginning of February, when the city was at its coldest and wettest, they found themselves alone together. Anthony had a new play to score and he stayed in most afternoons to work. Paige kept to her own office on the first floor and bothered him as little as possible, for she was terrified of him.

Paige had always considered her aunt Agnes her favorite aunt and had honored her as such, but never with any expectations of patronage. Now she felt blessed beyond her most extravagant fantasies and in spite of the stress of holding such an important position, she looked forward joyfully to work each day. And everything seemed to be going smoothly at the Greenwich Village brownstone by her lights, until that particular day when Anthony caught her reading Frank and I at lunch.

She wondered at first whether he disapproved of erotica, because it seemed to her that he began to find fault with her from then on. The very next morning he called her into his study to criticize everything about her. He told her to make an appointment at Sassoon that afternoon and spend the rest of the day at Saks. He had called ahead to his favorite sales woman, who would be ready to equip Paige as befitted his secretary.

Paige looked down at her black and white polka dot rayon dress and uninspired black flats, blushing as only a person of Celtic extraction can. In fact, her face became so hot with shame that he feared she might faint or burst into tears, but he hardened his heart and merely stared back at her.

"Yes, Paige, I don't know what you could possibly do to look more dowdy, but I'm afraid that if you're allowed to go unchecked much longer, you'll think of something."

"But, Mr. Newton, I can't afford a shopping spree at Saks or a haircut at Sassoon's."

"I can."

"You'd do that for me?"

"For me, Paige. I'm an aesthete. Hadn't you noticed? Now get going. And don't forget to get a manicure. Bitten fingernails are forbidden from now on."

After looking up the word aesthete, Paige left the house, an ordinary girl in a purple down overcoat, to return four hours later, with Dennis in the Bentley, laden with packages, a sleek, smart, shiny capped brunette, with sheer Calvin Klein underpinnings against her soft, pink skin and DKNY on top, the puffy parka replaced by a beautifully cut tweed coat with a matching cloche.

The transformation was as Anthony had expected. "We still have to get you a couple of pair of new glasses," he decided, adding, "I'd better go with you and help you pick."

"But, Mr. Newton, is this really important enough for you to spend your incredibly precious time on?" Paige was incredulous.

"I just want to make sure you don't make a terrible mistake like when you bought those," he said, leading her out to the street.

When the glasses had been selected he spent the time while they were waiting to receive them in buying her a leather briefcase and good pen. Finally she was properly outfitted to be taken to lunch and not embarrass him, he remarked bluntly. Again that high color, which had been so frightening the first time he saw it, flooded her face, though lunch proved thrilling from her point of view.

After that she thought he would be satisfied with the changes, but he wasn't nearly done. So far they had just seen to the cosmetic flaws. There was still the unfortunate accent to be dealt with and Anthony was for hiring a speech teacher to help.

"But, Mr. Newton," she protested, "that seems like a ridiculous expenditure. After all, I'm not an actress."

"Do you want to be my secretary for many years to come?" he asked.

"Yes!"

"It would help if I enjoyed the sound of your voice."

"Oh!"

The lessons began the following day. At first Paige was mortified, but as her diction began to improve, she embraced the English language.

As Anthony came to know her, he quickly decided that her spirit was too weak and her intellectual scope too narrow to seriously interest him as a lover. He was drawn to adventurous women and Paige was a mouse. However, having determined that she had no objection to being remodeled, he went about the business of developing her taste and discernment with vim.

The fact that she had a cheerfully malleable disposition helped a great deal. Paige was always ready to yield to the will of a stronger personality, as long as she wasn't being asked to do anything too risky. It took him a couple of weeks to recognize this characteristic and it interested him. Her innate submissiveness combined with her appealing looks and eagerness to please would have qualified her as an attractive potential playmate, had her personality been more determined. And yet there was something very pleasant about Paige's soft, undemanding presence. He especially enjoyed the sweet, unadulterated scent of her sensitive, never perfumed skin.

On the other hand, it was her very mildness that most often annoyed him. She was the least aggressive career woman he had ever met. She had no conception of her position and almost fainted when she saw her first paycheck. This was what caused her the greatest anxiety whenever she made a mistake.

One night when it was very cold, she reverted to the purple parka on the way home.

"I thought I told you to get rid of that coat," Anthony said, running into her in the hall and causing her to instantly redden with embarrassment.

"But it's a long walk to the train, Mr. Newton," she explained. "And it's cold out there!"

"Train? You take the subway home?"

"Of course," she laughed.

"After dark? That can't be safe. How far is it to the station?"

"Four blocks."

"From now on Dennis can drive you home," he said, calling his driver on the house phone.

Paige was frightened by this honor but heart swelled with pride each time the handsome, English, uniformed driver opened the door of the Bentley for her.

As much as he spoiled her, Anthony criticized and corrected Paige. It was easy to do. She was remarkably unsophisticated for a native New Yorker. She was intelligent, but lacked the subtlety. Her tastes were banal and she epitomized the ordinary. However, when he reflected on how quiet and utterly respectful Paige was, and how competently she did her work, Anthony did not regret his decision to take her on. She also had begun to worship him and this made for a contented employee. Her sheer happiness at arriving at her pretty little study each morning was almost more than she could bear and she hated to leave at night.

Perhaps she did not fully realize what an important position she herself held, but Paige did know that she was working for a star, who, (though they inhabited the same space at certain times during the day), moved in an entirely different sphere than most mortals. In short, Paige never forgot her place while quickly becoming a trusted confidante. She was the perfect sounding board. Her suggestions, when ventured, were intuitive and moderate. She was sensitive, judicious and kind. But in certain respects Paige was far from practical and even exhibited a tendency to engage in ritualistic behavior, which Anthony could only classify, as idiotic.

They had their first actual dispute over her yearly Tarot reading. Anthony told her it was nonsense and superstition while Paige attempted to staunchly defend the science of divination. Her arguments, however, lacked eloquence, and he interrupted her half way through it to inform Paige that she deserved a good spanking for wasting money on fortunetellers. This statement was received with the most frightening blush he'd seen on her so far. The color simply flooded her face in an instant.

"Oh, never mind," he quickly said, dismissing the entire conversation as he noted the sensational effect his casual comment had had on her. "Go on to your reading. I'll deprogram you some other time."

Paige escaped in a state of embarrassment and confusion. She felt that although he was kind, he despised her for not being brighter.

The next morning Paige somberly reported to Anthony that she had cancelled her reading and would not be scheduling another. For the truth was, after he had spoken of the Tarot with such contempt, respecting him as she did, she could no longer hold the cards in high regard.

Anthony, who was relieved that she had received his scolding in the spirit in which it was intended, softened at her sad humility.

"I hope you weren't offended by my mentioning a spanking," he smiled at her over the morning's mail. This casual remark instantly evoked the crimson blush. Her dark blue eyes flashed at him momentarily, then dropped to her shoes.

"No, sir," she quickly replied. Then added, with the first mischievous smile he had ever received from her, "That would be a pleasure, coming from you."

"Would it now?" he folded his arms and scrutinized her.

At that moment the phone rang and Paige picked it up with relief. After a moment she said, "Yes, Ma'am, may I tell him who's calling?"

Anthony frowned when she mentioned the name of his least favorite ex-wife. He took the phone but before speaking he covered the receiver and told Paige to come back in ten minutes.

When Paige returned in the appointed time Anthony was off the phone but still seated behind his desk. "Paige, what did I tell you about answering calls when I'm in?"

Paige instantly flushed, aware that she had done something wrong but not sure of what it had been.

"Did I forget something?" her legs turned to rubber at his stern, appraising glance.

"What did you say when the call from my ex-wife came in?"

"I said: May I tell him who's calling," Paige recalled, terrified that she was gong to be fired.

"That's right. Now, I understand that its easy to become flustered when confronted with the insistent voice of an ex-wife, but that's no excuse for forgetting your basic office etiquette, is it, Paige?"

"No, Sir," she replied, trembling with mortification.

"What should you have said to my ex-wife?"

"Just a moment, I'll see if he's in?" she asked.

"No, save that for people I might possibly want to talk to. Everyone else should be told that I've gone out."

"I understand."

"And naturally I'm always in to Susan or her sister."

"I'm terribly sorry, Mr. Newton," she murmured.

"You should be. Because of you I had to talk to Gloria for seven and a half minutes."

"I'm sorry."

"Don't look so terrified, Paige, you're only getting a spanking," he said, getting up, taking her firmly by the forearm over to the tufted leather sofa under the window and adroitly turning her over his knee. Anthony positioned her slender bulk correctly across his lap and smoothed down her skirt over her perfect oval buttocks.

"Young lady, you're about to discover just how long seven and a half minutes can be," he told her before bringing the palm of his hand down on her bottom.

Paige was breathlessly astonished. This was so sudden, so

intimate, so deliriously exciting. Nothing like this ever happened to Paige, whose unremarkable sexual history could be told in a paragraph. His hard palm descending to warm the seat of her tight, gray tweed skirt produced a voluptuous sting, which felt anything but painful to the receptive girl.

And then, before she knew it, it was over. He was setting her back on her feet with her heart still wildly thumping. Had seven plus minutes really passed? She almost cried with frustration on being released, so charming had it felt to lie across his lap and feel his hand on her waist while he spanked her. Unconsciously she reached back to rub her bottom while she gazed at him with wide eyes.

"Now let that be a lesson to you, young lady," he recommended, returning to his desk.

Paige returned to her office in a daze. When he looked in on her a little later in the afternoon she was sitting with her chin on her hand, staring into space.

"Paige! What are you daydreaming about? Don't you have something to do?" he startled her into one of her now famous terror blushes.

"Yes sir," she sat up straight and returned to her typing immediately. He left her with a smile, enchanted with her compliance, which permitted her to submit to such liberties as he had taken with quiet pleasure.

For several weeks Paige relived the poignant seven and a half minutes she had spent across Anthony's lap with exquisite joy. As unsophisticated as she was, Paige understood that this attention, which he had bestowed upon her, was much more a mark of favor than displeasure. For Dennis had confided to her once on the drive home from work, that Mr. Newton had a tendency to be somewhat strict with his little Susan, and that on more than one occasion, Dennis had overheard the distinctive sound of a spanking being administered to that adorable young lady by their boss.

Once Paige met Susan and saw her together with Anthony, she couldn't stop fantasizing about those occasions when Anthony might be provoked into disciplining his blonde, blue eyed, Ivy League coed.

It was terrifically exciting just being in the same room with the two of them and being able to watch their subtle body language. Once Paige came in while Susan was leaving and she caught a glimpse of their parting kiss and the resounding smack he gave the seat of her jeans as she departed. This tiny episode stayed with Paige for weeks, causing her tummy to clench with excitement every time she remembered it.

Because of her ability to listen, Anthony shared many of his thoughts with Paige. He enjoyed talking about Susan and Paige listened with rapt attention. Some of Susan's letters from school about her new boyfriend Marcus Gower, Anthony read aloud to Paige, to get her opinion of the developing situation. Paige was shocked and thought it terrible that Susan was sharing her favors with anyone other than her devoted lover. But Anthony smiled at her alarm, confident that the only way to handle Susan was to let her do exactly as she pleased.

Towards the end of February, Anthony was scheduled to take a trip Los Angeles for a week to sell the film rights to one of his shows. The details had already been worked out, with the studio visit being merely a formality, but he was looking forward to the trip for other reasons. He had never played in the L.A. scene before and eagerly anticipated meeting a special young lady he'd followed in magazines and videos for years.

Against his better judgment, he brought Paige with him on the trip. Her complete lack of industry protocol made her almost more of a liability than an asset on the status conscious West Coast, but he needed her to handle the smaller details of the trip, which he had no time for.

Dennis was also brought along to drive them and they all stayed at the Beverly Wilshire Hotel. Paige, who was a simple girl, easily thrilled by all forms of shallow entertainment, was in ecstasy at being in California for the first time, with her boss, whom she adored, staying at the same hotel that Richard Gere stayed at in Pretty Woman; and to make it even more fantastic, she had one whole day off to go to Disneyland. Anthony had Dennis take her there. (He was fond of Paige, but not that fond.)

Meanwhile, he himself had a date, with a beautiful professional submissive named Teresa Clifford. Teresa was a clever, sophisticated and sexually magnetic brunette in her early thirties, who had appeared in numerous bondage and spanking videos. She had been drawing and writing a B&D comic strip for Hugo Sands' publication for several years and also maintained a semi-legitimate freelance career, writing and cartooning for a handful of alternative newspapers and magazines. Anthony had all of her videos and copies of every piece she had ever published and had been looking forward to meeting her for several years, though it was only recently he'd learned that she was available for private sessions.

Anthony arrived at the door of her modest Beverly Hills apartment in the highest spirits. Nor was he disappointed when she opened the door, a graceful girl with a bisque complexion and a long, thick, jet-black ponytail, dressed in a black leather cat suit, which well became her sculpted body. She was of medium height, with an extremely beautiful bosom and bottom, each of which were perfectly rounded, high and pert. Her bracelets and earrings were onyx edged with gold, her lips and nails dark red, her lace up ankle boots had 4" heels. The outfit would have been equally acceptable at Spago or a B&D club.

Anthony inhaled a faint scent of exotic perfume as he followed her inside, feeling as comfortable with Teresa as if he'd known her for years, which indeed he had, through her clever quips on film and trenchant observations in print.

Her visitor, on the other hand, immediately and completely nonplused Teresa. She knew him only as Anthony Marshall, which was the name he used when he played in the scene, a gracious and articulate businessman who sent her Parisian chocolates on Valentine's Day and silk satin lingerie at Christmas, just because he enjoyed her work. He had written her several fan letters over the past few years, to which she had duly responded with brief, polite notes of thanks, adding one or two additional comments to indicate her personal enjoyment of hazelnut truffles and Fernando Sanchez teddies.

He had called her for the first time the previous month and had politely arranged for this meeting. She knew from the tone and content of his letters that he was an unpretentious dominant with a spanking fetish that found her appealing. He hadn't made a murmur at her fee and had sent a large bouquet of yellow roses to her that morning. Teresa had never been courted quite so lavishly, yet as pleasing as these considerations were, she did not anticipate the evening with any particular excitement, since she had no idea of what he might look like or even how old he might be.

However, her attitude changed the moment she opened the door to this really handsome and quite youthful gentleman in an impeccably tailored suit.

"Anthony?" she seemed dazed as she showed him in.

"Teresa, I'm so happy to meet you at last." He shook her hand.

"I'm happy to meet you too," Teresa said sincerely. "And thank you for all the wonderful presents."

"Let's get this out of the way now," he said, handing her an envelope.

"Okay. Thanks," she said. "Would you excuse me a minute? Please, help yourself to a drink," Teresa went into her bedroom to put the money away. Peeking in the envelope, she saw that that he had put in double what she'd asked him.

When Teresa came out she looked troubled. "Does this mean you're going to be extra hard?"

Anthony laughed at her concern and commented on her record and tape collection, which he'd been looking at while she was away. "Do you listen to nothing but Gershwin, Harold Arlen and Kurt Weill?" he asked her.

"I am partial to that era," she admitted.

"Do you know this one?" he asked her, sitting down at her old upright piano and playing That Certain Feeling in the fast and exuberant style in which the composer himself had played. Had she closed her eyes she might have fancied herself listening to an original piano roll.

Now Teresa was truly stunned. Did she dream him? He had even picked her favorite song.

"Anthony, are you a professional pianist?"

"Something like that," he replied with a smile. She suddenly seemed to realize that she was with an important person and this distracted her completely for a moment or two. Then she remembered the purpose of his visit and actually blushed. Anthony noticed and came to sit beside her on the sofa.

"Scared?" he asked her.

"Yes."

"Why?"

"Sometimes handsome men are extra hard."

"Oh, I'm sure I'll be extra hard by the time I'm through with you," he said, patting her sleek thigh through the leather cat suit. Seeing that she was at a loss as to how to proceed he took control, telling her that they would grab a bite at Le Chardonnay and then she could take him to the best-equipped dungeon in the city so they could play.

However, before they went out the door, Anthony took her over his knee and spanked her very firmly a few dozen times for wearing the glamorous but inconvenient cat suit.

"Young lady," he told her sternly, "I want you to learn a lesson from this spanking. When you meet a dominant man for a date and you know he's been dreaming about your bottom for years, you do not wear an outfit which renders that flawless object virtually inaccessible to his hand."

More spanks followed, setting Teresa on fire. Then she suddenly remembered something pertinent.

"Anthony? I can explain about the cat suit."

"Oh?" he stayed his hand.

"Yes, you see there's an OOTC party tonight that I was planning to attend in case you cancelled."

"OOTC? What's that?"

"Out Of The Closet. It's the local B&D support group. Tonight is one of their quarterly parties. We can go if you like. I'm a member," she leaned up on his thigh to tell him this. Anthony thought this was a fine idea and let her up. Teresa looked at him with wide eyes, still rubbing her bottom and not moving for several seconds.

"Yes? You have something to say?" he pulled her hands away from her bottom and held them, looking up at her. Teresa flushed and felt very excited.

"No, sir," she replied and went to get her jacket. She was in love.

Teresa drove her older BMW convertible, rapidly and recklessly, through Beverly Hills with Anthony in the front seat beside her, eyeing her with horror every block or so. After one near miss she shouted out her window at an aggressively driven male-owned Mercedes convertible, "Fucking asshole!"

Anthony calmly took out a small leather pocket notebook and made a jot.

"What?" she looked at him and laughed. "What are you doing?"

"You get three marks for reckless driving and two for discourtesy," he informed her, putting the book away.

"He fucking cut me off!" Anthony took the book out again.

"Two more for vulgarity. You know better words, Teresa."

"Look, you don't understand, you're from New York."

"So are you, judging from your accent."

"I know. But I'm out here now."

"Teresa?"

"Yes, Anthony?"

"Would you like to see me again the next time I come into town?"

"Sure!" she said with sincerity.

"Then don't kill me this time, damn it!"

Teresa laughed but didn't decrease her speed as she zipped over to the restaurant.

During dinner he couldn't resist asking Teresa whether she also enjoyed contemporary musicals. For a moment, at the split second he said the word musical, he almost looked familiar to her, as though she ought to know him from somewhere.

"You never did send me your picture before, did you?" she asked.

"No."

"I just suddenly got the feeling I'd seen you before. Are you famous?"

"Would you be better behaved if I told you I was?" he teased her.

"Probably," she replied honestly, accepting a glass of champagne. "But what did you just ask me?"

"Whether you liked modern Broadway shows."

"Oh! No. I really don't. Do you?"

"Well, I..."

"I mean, what's out there besides Andrew Lloyd Weber's overblown tedium and Anthony Newton's insubstantial fluff?"

"Yes, I do see your point," he agreed, refilling her glass.

The OOTC party was on Las Palmas Street off Hollywood Boulevard. They parked in a large lot beside the meeting hall. Teresa told him to be careful, as this wasn't a good neighborhood.

He paid for their admissions at the door. Everyone knew Teresa. Inside the walls were painted black and the rooms were packed with roving, leather-clad players. They walked through the rooms together, taking in the various scenes. A whipping here, a clothes pin application to the nipples there, a spanking in the corner, etc., with leather harnesses on every other male. Virtually everyone wore black. In fact, Anthony was conspicuous in his summer weight khaki suit.

One of the rooms had a small stage surrounded by tiers of theatrical seating. On the stage a man was whipping a voluptuous, nearly nude girl who was bound to an X-frame while twenty or so men and women watched. Her breasts were enrobed in clothespins, a ball gag filled her mouth and a blindfold wrapped her eyes.

Many people stopped Teresa to talk to her as they went through the rooms, including her friend Jesse, a slim, sexy, submissive lawyer in her late thirties, who ground up against Teresa almost immediately and begged for a strapping.

"Please, Mistress, Teresa. I need it now!" said the shameless young woman, smiling at Anthony in the naughtiest possible way. "Take me in the bathroom and bend me over the sink?"

Jesse was slender, with a small bust and dainty waist, now displayed to advantage by a black silk bustier and matching skirt over lacing Victorian boots. Her jet-black hair and white skin matched Teresa's and the girls looked very sisterly walking off together arm in arm. Anthony could tell by the look of recognition in Jesse's eyes that this girl who talked like a hooker but like himself, wore a Yale signet ring, knew exactly whom he was.

Once they were alone in the bathroom Jesse was more curious than horny for once. "Honey, you are moving in exalted circles these days!"

"I am? Oh, my date. Yes, isn't he delicious? I don't want to leave him alone out there too long because he's so cute that someone might steal him. But, where do you know him from?"

"I don't know him from anywhere, but I've seen every one of his shows."

"You mean, his concert performances?" Teresa asked, still under the impression her date was a concert pianist.

"I mean all of Anthony Newton's hit Broadway shows." And Jesse went on to recite their names.

"Anthony Newton?" Teresa repeated dumbly, feeling her knees turn to sand. "That's him?"

"Didn't you know?" Jesse laughed.

"I thought his name was Anthony Marshall. We're actually doing a session tonight." Teresa touched up her lipstick with a sinking feeling. "And I just insulted the hell out of him."

"Really? He doesn't look the slightest bit offended. He's very rich, you know. I had no idea he was in the scene."

"Don't tell anyone."

"I won't," Jesse lied.

"I'd better get back. I'll deal with your insatiable libido some other time."

"I understand, honey. Tell him he can bend me over the car and give me a strapping in the parking lot in fifteen minutes."

True to her word, Jesse came outside and with Teresa standing between them and the vacant security guard, the mischievous brunette allowed Anthony to pull up her skirt and apply the end of his belt to her black pantied bottom six times hard as she ground against the hood of the BMW. He pulled the panties up into her crack for the last three to reveal her shapely white cheeks joined to smooth thighs, which were bare above her stockings. Jesse made sounds as though she were climaxing, but Teresa told him later that she always did that to clear up any confusion as to whether or not she was a slut.

After Jesse went back inside, Teresa lit a cigarette and leaned up against the fender of her car, like the girls used to do back in New York in the old neighborhoods. Anthony also took a cigarette and was still smiling at the thought of sexy, demanding little Jesse when Teresa began a stumbling and painful apology for her ill-advised remarks about Anthony Newton.

"Don't worry about it," he told her reassuringly. "I have plenty of fans. In our relationship, I'm your fan."

"But I feel so mortified. It was such an insensitive assessment of a really... admirable body of work."

"Better quit while you're ahead, Teresa."

"Anthony, I fully understand if you want to call the session off and I'll be happy to return the money," she suggested meekly.

"Scared?" he seemed amused.

"Damn it, I just feel bad for saying what I did. I mean, you're a genius. Everyone knows that." The black ponytail swung with emphasis.

Anthony sighed and leveled a serious glance at her for the first time. "Teresa?"

"Yes, Anthony?"

"Give me the keys and get in. I'll drive."

They drove over Laurel Canyon to a famous B&D club in the Valley, where they rented the best-equipped room for an hour. The first thing he did was to zip Teresa out of her cat suit and then put the ankle boots back on her. Once he had her stripped down to a pair of black French cut lace briefs and a décolleté bra, he wasted no time in seating himself on the leather padded bondage bed and taking her across his lap for a sound spanking. In due time the panties came down to reveal one of the most perfect bottoms he had ever exposed.

The next phase began with Anthony telling her to bring him a paddle, a strap, a whip and a wooden hairbrush; He then removed his jacket, loosened his tie and rolled up his sleeves. He added that he wanted her naked except for her shoes. Taking her back across his lap he scolded her thoroughly for her arrogance and lack of tact and gave her a dozen resounding smacks with the paddle on her bare bottom. Teresa kicked and cried out with shock and pain, nearly sobbing towards the end, but neither protested or struggled to break free of his grip on her waist. She felt she had this coming.

"You did insult me," he told her, "but that's not as great a sin in my eyes as the untuned piano." He now took up the hairbrush and laid on an additional twelve smacks. "I want that piano tuned next time I come back to L.A. Understand me, young lady?" These swats were lighter than those he'd given her with the paddle and merely stung.

"Yes, sir!" she meekly tried to put one hand back to shield her bottom, but he pushed it firmly away.

"Then there are the marks against you for the reckless driving." Anthony reached for the short strap she had taken off the wall for their use.

For the strapping he made her bend over a padded horse with her legs straight and together. The hairbrush and paddle had caused a dark rose blush to suffuse the unblemished skin of her well-rounded bottom, though he'd not used either implement with extreme force.

He pressed down with one hand in the small of her back while he strapped her bottom smartly about ten times. She took the strapping well, reacting charmingly to each stroke while occasionally turning her melting brown eyes towards him.

Suddenly it felt uncomfortably close in the dungeon. Anthony lay the strap aside and pulled her to her feet. As she turned to face him the sight of her upstanding, rosy nippled breasts, and her silky sable muff, so innocently inviting, greatly increased his passion for Teresa.

"You're having quite an effect on me," he confessed, gently pressing her hand to the bar of steel behind his zipper. Teresa purred with pleasure.

"You can do whatever you like," she told him, impulsively putting her arms around his neck and pressing her body against his.

"You wouldn't object to becoming more intimate?" he asked her, turning her around so that her back was pressed against his front. Then he held her tightly against him with one hand on her exquisite waist and the other enclosing her Venus mound. His lips brushed her throat.

"I'd like that more than anything," she ground back against him.

"Me too, but not here. Get dressed and we'll go back to my hotel."

"Goody!" she jumped up and jiggled.

"Maybe stop at The Pleasure Chest on the way?"

"Oh? What for, Anthony?" she had herself zipped back into her cat suit in ten seconds.

"Couple of vibrators, some Astroglide and a small flogger," he replied coolly.

"And some condoms," she added.

The next morning Anthony awoke with a smile, remembering the pleasures of the night before, though he was shocked to realize that it was already nine and immediately called Paige, who had also overslept and sounded groggy.

"Paige, where's my breakfast?" he impulsively demanded, as though the matter had been previously discussed.

"Breakfast?" she answered with surprise.

"And where's the barber and the manicurist?"

"Barber?" Paige echoed dumbly, making no attempt to conceal her amazement.

"Paige, did you forget that I have an appointment at the studio this afternoon?"

"No, sir," Paige answered shakily, sitting up in the luxurious black walnut bed with a guilty start.

"Didn't you realize that you're here to take care of those little details for me?" Anthony sounded seriously annoyed.

"I'm sorry, Mr. Newton. I'll call for the barber right away."

"Don't forget the manicurist and my breakfast. I want scrambled eggs, toast and coffee. Okay?"

"Yes, sir, I'm terribly sorry," Paige appeared to be on the verge of tears. When she hung up the phone she nearly felt out of bed in her rush to disentangle herself from the opulent linens, which upholstered it.

Paige appeared in his room in twenty minutes, washed, brushed and combed, in a beige linen sheath and ankle strap espadrilles. All her California outfits had been personally approved by Anthony, to her great humiliation, lest she embarrass him. She did not look happy.

"Give me the good news first," he told her, over folded arms. Her confusion was adorable. Perhaps it was the balmy Southern California air after the bitter cold of a New York winter, but Anthony felt the blood racing in his veins that morning.

"The good news is that breakfast is on the way," Paige said, then took a deep breath before admitting, "the bad news is that the barber and manicurist here in the hotel are booked all morning."

"Did you ask for someone else?"

"They gave me a list of salons in Beverly Hills. But Mr. Newton, they charge a fortune to come out," Paige revealed, as though this fact caused the subject to be irrevocably closed.

"Paige, that's not a problem. Get someone out right away."

"But, Mr. Newton, remember how they charged President Clinton two hundred dollars for a haircut?"

"Paige, didn't I just tell you to get someone out here?"

"Yes, sir," she turned to leave, believing her boss had gone mad.

"Paige?"

"Yes, sir?"

"What were you doing so late last night that you overslept?"

Paige blushed dreadfully. "Nothing, sir."

"Tell me."

"Well, after Disneyland, Dennis and I went to an English bar called the Cat and Fiddle in Hollywood. And we got a little bit loaded. Then we just came back here."

"And?"

"And, I guess we drank a little more after that in my room."

"Is that all you did, Paige?"

"We talked quite a lot. And Dennis rubbed my feet. They were so sore after Disneyland."

"H'm, I'll bet. Well, all of this is most improper, you know that, don't you?"

"Improper?"

"Call for the barber then come back here. We're going to address the subject of fraternization."

Paige left all atremble, unable to decide whether he was really angry, momentarily cross or simply teasing her. Of course she hadn't been able to get up on time that morning. She was completely thrown off schedule from jet lag. She'd never traveled so far on a plane before. Furthermore, going to bed in the magnificent room, after an evening of the most indulgently respectful attentions from the handsome young driver, had put her into a state of subtle ecstasy, so that when the sun filtered in through the French doors that morning, she naturally thought she was dreaming and went peacefully back to sleep.

After ordering the ridiculously expensive hair stylist and

manicurist, Paige tried desperately to remember whether she had ever been told by Anthony to order breakfast or a barber.

In spite of her fear and shame, she joined him again and remained in his suite the whole time he had breakfast, had his hair trimmed and his nails buffed. He looked at her from time to time with a cool, stern look of appraisal that made her stomach clench with a mixture of anxiety and excitement.

When everyone had left it was still only noon and Anthony didn't have to leave for an hour, so he decided to amuse himself with Paige. After looking over the messages and faxes that had come in since breakfast, he turned all of his attention to the nervous girl.

He had her sit on one of the love seats in the vast parlor of his suite. She didn't dare meet his eyes.

"What am I going to do with you?"

She bit her lip and compulsively twiddled her thumbs, her entire body an arrow of tension. A sudden twinge of conscience stuck him silent. While he decided how to deal with it, he went behind her and massaged the back of her neck. "Relax," he told her, deftly unkinking her neck. "You're not in that much trouble." Paige visibly untensed almost immediately, looking up at him over one smooth shoulder with immense gratitude.

"I'm not?"

"Put your head down," he told her. She groaned with pleasure as the massage continued. Then she lifted her head with a guilty start.

"Mr. Newton, you shouldn't be doing this."

"No?"

Paige withdrew her slim shoulders from his grasp and changed her seat, looking embarrassed again.

"You know, Paige, I was just wondering how badly you'd blush if I pulled your panties down next time I spanked you."

Anthony received an answer in the form of a color. "I'm sure you agree that you deserve a good spanking for getting drunk with the hired help and oversleeping this morning."

Paige looked up at him with her guileless blue eyes and replied, "Yes, sir." She looked so sweetly submissive at that moment that it was almost impossible for him to believe that she wasn't fully and completely in the scene. He almost burst out, "Are you into it, or not?" but didn't, because he was afraid of finding out that Paige was merely adoringly simple and would naturally submit to a spanking or anything else her idol suggested.

His lively animal spirits encouraged him to press his advantage and dominate the naturally compliant girl completely, while his feminist-friendly alter ego shrieked in horror at the liberty he was about to take with his unquestioningly obedient employee.

But why kid himself, he was about to do a slightly wicked thing. Something had decided him that morning. He was on holiday, she was delicious and he knew in his heart that she longed to be handled by him. Perhaps she wasn't truly in the scene, but some girls you had to bring into the scene. They weren't all brilliant self-starters. Some girls didn't even realize they were into it until some other person introduced them to it. At least, so he had heard.

"Well," he said briskly, "I'm glad you agree with me. However, since I don't have time to give you a proper spanking now, come over here," he commanded. She hesitated only slightly, then came to him and allowed him to bend her over a massive marble table. Then he took off his belt and wound the buckle portion around his hand. She caught her breath as he placed his other hand in the small of her back to hold her in place. "But I do have time to give you a licking."

He administered six moderate strokes of the strap across her skirt, just hard enough to get her attention. The strokes were slightly sharp and to Paige, felt purely sexual. The strap bewitched her. She steeled herself for a second volley, squeezing her eyes shut like a small child awaiting a severe paddling. But instead he pulled her back up to her feet.

"That's enough for now," he told her; "Tell Dennis we'll be leaving in ten minutes."

Paige exited with a scarlet face, wondering how she could possibly concentrate on the important meeting to follow. Anthony meanwhile reflected on how close he'd just come to possibly making a dreadful mistake with a girl he hardly knew. Was he really about to bare her bottom? After administering the six he had felt very warm. He was becoming intensely excited by the look of Paige bent over, her sweetly trusting face and her obvious submissiveness.

Then all at once he thought of Mrs. O'Conner, Paige's aunt. What would she think of the way he was treating her niece, whom she had brought to him in good faith? He remembered newspaper clippings telling of Southern attorneys whose reputations had been destroyed because they had given in to the outlandish impulse to spank their secretaries.

Naturally, this situation was somewhat different, but just as sticky. Paige was no seventeen-year-old temp who had bent over for him because she didn't know any better. She had assumed the position with an attitude of trust and breathless expectation. He had other indications that she was intrigued by dominance and submission. There was the famous Edwardian novel he'd found her reading, which became more significant combined with her admission that a spanking from him would be a pleasure. But these trifles were not enough to lead him to suppose that he'd found a player.

If he had been able to believe with conviction, that Paige really liked being treated like a child, he wouldn't hesitate to keep the girl in a constant state of heat, but he had no way of knowing exactly what her true feelings were. Paige, with her feudal submissiveness, never would presume to articulate her feelings about those few exquisite moments when he had chosen to discipline her, without being specifically questioned about them.

Anthony was troubled about the developing situation with Paige because there was the danger that she was simply falling in love with her boss. Her tractability was charming and he was sure her bottom must be beautiful, but did he really intend to become her master? This sort of behavior was not like him. And yet her softness was beginning to enchant him. She seemed a perfect play toy, receptive in every way and with no actual agenda of her own to impede their progress together. But how could he prevent her from falling in love? This seemed the impossible task.

He thought of this problem instead of the movie deal on the way over to the studio. Paige sat quietly and looked at the gates of Bel Air gliding past the window of the limousine. Her color had faded to a dusky rose. She didn't dare meet his eyes. Every few minutes she would mentally relive the short strapping and feel a thrill.

"That's where the Reagans live, Paige," he told her; because he knew that sort of fact fascinated her. She looked as pleased as a child. Her innocence pierced him and for the first time he felt a pang of real conscience.

"Paige, dear, you know I wouldn't tease you if I didn't like you, don't you?"

Paige instantly gave him her full attention. Then she smiled.

"You do tease me a lot," she said.

"And you're such a good sport about it too. But it suddenly occurred to me that perhaps I'd gone too far."

"Oh, no!"

"My language in the suite just now, I recall was quite shocking, to say nothing of my actions, which would have given extreme offense to the majority of employees."

"Oh!" Paige looked at him with wide eyes. "You mean..."

"Yes, the strapping."

"Well, I didn't find it offensive, Mr. Newton. Just the opposite actually, thank you," she said with a quickly coloring face.

"You're blushing terribly, Paige," Anthony observed coolly, though inwardly delighted by her frank admission, "Do you plan to go into the meeting like that?"

"I'm sorry, it was the topic."

"Yes, but suppose I happen to look at you during the meeting and you happen to remember the topic. Are you going to blush like that?"

"I'll try not to."

The remainder of the trip proved so hectic, as well as the first few days after they returned to New York, that Anthony had no further opportunities to explore this interesting new facet of his secretary's character. Indeed, it was the only interesting aspect of Paige he had noticed so far, so why should he not help her develop it? If she were indeed as submissive as he thought she was, he would be doing her an immense favor in introducing her to the scene, with all of its eligible bachelors.

Certainly he'd heard nothing about a boyfriend, and girls like Paige always chattered night and day about their boyfriends to anyone who would listen, if they had them. But why stop at a boyfriend? With her looks and tractability, he could find her a rich husband in a matter of months. Her entire life might be transformed, if it was true that she was really into it.

Viewing the situation from this prospective was much more agreeable to Anthony. She would be his project. He would bring her out. Meanwhile, she would receive some additional allowance for the liberties he knew he could not prevent himself from taking, her attitude being what it was.

The first time she received a heavier envelope she went straight to her boss to report the error. Anthony explained that no mistake had been made. He had simply made her a present because she did so well on the trip to California. Paige left his study confused, knowing full well that she had just barely managed to stagger through the trip to California. Never the less, being a sensible girl, she argued no further.

Paige was by no means as simple as he thought her. For instance, she had figured out by now that he liked her, really liked her. It was apparent in his words, deeds and body language. And this gave her the courage to finally speak a few well-chosen thoughts aloud to him. It took many weeks for the perfect moment, as what Paige had to say was of a precise and delicate nature. It required his complete and undivided attention, and of course, the best possible mood. It had to be brought up on a day when he himself took a moment or two out to ask her how things were going or simply chat. So that the focus was already on her. And then she could bring it up.

The right moment came on a frigid Thursday night in late February, when the wind was blowing furiously enough to rattle the windows in the old brick house. Anthony had taken a break from working on his new libretto to visit Paige in her office where she was responding to correspondence. He came in, picked up the letter, which had just come out of the printer and scanned it for errors, which frightened her profoundly. But her training at Macy's had served her well and her style of correspondence was properly polite and cool headed.

"Good," he said, "but I'd run it through the spell checker."

"I will," she replied with embarrassment. He smiled at her. "But it's okay otherwise, right?"

"Oh, fine," he said pleasantly, noticing how prettily her full skirted, fringed, beige wool dress fit her slender body. "How are you doing, sweetheart?"

"Me? Oh, fine. Thank you," she said quickly, looking at him with a beating heart.

"Good."

"Mr. Newton? Do you have a minute?"

"Sure."

"Can I speak to you about something?"

"Of course." Anthony sat down on the chair alongside her desk and leaned his chin on his hand, frightening her with his complete attention. She sat back in her chair and began with difficulty.

"This is going to sound funny."

Anthony could see that Paige was groping for the right words and his own heart fluttered, as he wondered whether she was about the give notice because of the liberties he'd been taking with her.

"Paige, just relax, take a deep breath and tell me what's on your mind," he said reassuringly.

"It's a subject that I've never discussed with anyone before. Because I've never met anyone who could even remotely understand what I was talking about."

"Oh?" Anthony sat up. It suddenly became obvious to him that she was not about to give notice, but rather make some startling confession about her intimate thoughts or desires. "Do proceed," he told her gently.

"You're so smart that you've probably guessed what I'm leading up to," she said hopefully.

"Could it be something about the strapping?" he asked helpfully.

The color flooded her face as never before but this didn't worry him.

"Yes. You see, I felt that you stopped too soon."

"You did, did you?" Anthony felt his own face growing warm. She felt he stopped too soon!

"You see, I've always had fantasies of being... spanked. But until I

64

came to work for you, it never happened."

"Fantasies? Always?"

"Ever since I can remember. Especially by my boss."

"Aw!" he made the sound reserved for kittens and infants. "I knew I should hire you for some reason that day," he mused. "It certainly wasn't your appearance or qualifications, though you've cleaned up handsomely and have proven competent."

"Thank you."

"Paige, why did you wait so long to tell me this?"

"You mean after the first time?" Paige blushed furiously now. "I guess because I wasn't sure it really happened. Don't laugh, Mr. Newton. It might have been a whim that overtook you that day. How could I know that you might truly understand me? But then, in California when you had me bend over the table... well, I just knew then that you must share this passion for discipline that I've had all my life. I've wanted to speak about it since then, but it's taken a while for me to get up the nerve."

This was a long speech for Paige and Anthony appreciated the care with which it had been framed. He began to wonder whether he had been doing her a disservice in thinking her so dull all this time, when perhaps it was only a natural modesty and reticence which blurred the luster of her intellect. At any rate, her sudden eloquence on his favorite subject seemed to increase her IQ spectacularly.

"Well, I'm glad you finally did tell me, Paige, because I can help you. Under my guidance you will meet the man of your dreams. And meanwhile I will provide the discipline you need."

"You will?" her heart ached with joy.

"That is correct. From now on you'll get a spanking every Friday night, whether you need it or not." The next day was Friday. "I'm going to give you some magazines to look at tonight and I want you to write yourself a personal ad. We'll mail it in tomorrow and within a couple of months you'll have a booming social life."

"Is that true?"

"You'll see."

The following afternoon Paige received her first over the knee, bare bottom spanking from Anthony. It lasted for a full half hour. He didn't spank her constantly, but paused now and then to massage and caress her exquisitely beautiful bottom. At the end he was spanking her very hard, but she was in such a state of euphoria that she barely felt the pain, although later she wondered at the ache. She was more aroused than she had ever been in her life. Her extremely fair skin had been stained a deep magenta pink by his hand. The spanking made her so wet that he was compelled to change his trousers.

Towards the end of the spanking, feeling that perhaps she was receiving too much enjoyment, she awkwardly offered to "do something else if he liked."

Anthony did not take this suggestion well. He firmly pointed out that theirs was to be a corporal punishment relationship; due to the fact the he already had a girlfriend. He spanked her hard, telling her that he expected her to behave like a lady and not a little slut. Paige sobbed and promised to behave while squirming against his hard thighs. In spite of the words he had spoken, Anthony deliberately intermixed digital penetration with spanking her until she achieved her first over the knee climax. After allowing her to recover her composure, Anthony made her stand in the corner with her skirt up, and scolded her about making improper advances to him, warning her that she'd get the hair brush spanking of her life if she ever tried to introduce sex into their discipline sessions again.

To Anthony's mind, masturbating a thrill-starved girl during a spanking did not count as sex and this was a way in which he could provide them both with pleasure without romantic complications. He did have the urge to consummate their scene in a lustier manner, but common sense restrained him. Knowing nothing of her emotional state, he couldn't risk turning their dominant /submissive relationship into a love affair which might break her heart.

Meanwhile, Paige began to diligently answer personal ads. Anthony obtained a P.O. Box for her use. He had a photographer take her portrait and had a hundred eight by ten glossies printed for her. He helped her write her ad, which finally read, "Single female, 31, submissive but discriminating, seeks financially secure, well educated, professional male late 20's - early 40's for dating relationship, featuring over the knee spankings. Prefer nurturing, young daddy type who will spoil and discipline me. Send photo, letter and phone to P.O. Box ___" Mostly it had been written by Anthony, based on his observations of his secretary. She loved the young daddy phrase, though she'd never thought of it that way before. She was also charmed by the black and white glossy of herself, which revealed how attractive she had become under Anthony's care.

He also taught her how to answer letters. He knew more about the scene and male motivations within it than she would have ever thought possible. He helped her weed out the useless replies and cultivate the promising ones.

When she had her first scene date he helped her choose her outfit and strategy. Late that night she called Anthony to report what had gone on. He listened with extreme interest and commended her at the conclusion. Paige hung up with a smile of wonder. For 31 years she had been a wallflower. Suddenly she had a glorious life, filled with adventure and excitement and sexual thrills beyond her most extravagant fantasies.

It was a long, quiet winter with Susan at school and the libretto to complete, so Anthony found himself alone in the house with Paige a good deal. This being the case it was almost impossible to restrict their playing to Friday afternoons. Indeed, he could not resist finding excuses to turn her over his knee three or four times a week.

The first few times it was very easy to simply spank her and let her go. But after a very short while the provocative sight of her fair Irish skin reddening under his hand mingled with her voluptuous scent and thrilling gyrations across his lap began to affect him severely.

He familiarized himself thoroughly with her sex, meticulously spreading her open, examining her petal by petal, and finally probing her velvety depths with gentle fingers. He knew her intimately, front and back, without ever taking her and it was beginning to frustrate him. Sometimes, after her spanking, he would hold her on his lap the right way around and firmly massage her flat tummy while fingering her and lightly spanking her pussy. This was another way he had found of making her climax.

Paige luxuriated in these attentions, but felt his need. Yet she remembered his injunction against having sex and refrained from addressing the subject for several encounters. Finally, however, when she could not help but notice as she lay across his lap one dark and stormy afternoon, how terribly hard his cock felt under her tummy, she made so bold as to speak on the subject again.

"Anthony?" she ventured timidly, over one shoulder, "Are you sure you don't want to do anything other than spank me today?"

He had indeed been thinking of nothing but splitting that smooth, round bottom with his cock for the very first time. But her tentative suggestion brought him to his senses.

"Paige, I've told you how I want our arrangement to work, haven't I?"

"Yes, sir."

"Then why are you trying to tempt me?" he stroked her glowing bottom deeply. "I'm going to punish you harshly for that."

And he did in fact administer twenty hard swats with the back of his wooden hairbrush to Paige, over her skirt, just before she went home, so she'd feel it sharply on the drive uptown.

Paige took the punishment in the spirit in which it was intended. She knew that her employer was trying very hard to be well behaved and she reproached herself for trying to change that. Besides, she had some other men to see, now that she was answering ads, and one or two of them had shown themselves to be highly willing to engage in sex after spanking.

The third time she tried to equalize the pleasure factor in their relationship was when she shyly offered to go down on him. In spite of the fact that his cock jumped in his trousers, Anthony resisted the impulse to take advantage of a girl he didn't love. Instead he walloped her firmly with a wide leather strap.

Anthony had indulged too much with Paige lately not to need some dramatic form of release. That same night he called Teresa Clifford and arranged to fly her out to New York for a few days. Even though it was a paid arrangement, he had loved Teresa from a distance for years, and that seemed to justify his lust.

Teresa arrived like a breath of warm, perfumed, desert air and he took her repeatedly, in the most romantic hotel in the city. He was surprised by how excited he felt at seeing Teresa again. He had repressed so much feeling about Paige these past few weeks that simply being able to speak freely about his sexual desires seemed liberating.

"You know, Teresa, you take too much in those videos you do," Anthony told her as they relaxed on a sofa with a view of snow capped Central Park stretching out below them through the windows of the suite. "I'm sure you're not getting paid enough to warrant canings and tears."

"Don't you enjoy canings and tears?"

"Yes, but my heart's gone out to you time and time again."

"It has?" Teresa had never heard anything like this before and was touched.

"I think that degree of severity may occasionally be appropriate between a girl and her lover or master, but I don't think you should give it away for every Tom, Dick and Harry to jack off to," he continued firmly.

"I agree, but if I'm doing a job, I have to be honorable, even if I don't have a crush on the administrator," Teresa explained.

"But so many of them have been unduly harsh with you," said Anthony, kissing the palm of her soft, white hand.

"Thank you for your compassion."

"I'm not saying that I haven't made my girlfriend cry once or twice. But unlike you, she deeply deserved it," Anthony suddenly confided.

"You spank your girlfriend?" Teresa was shocked and fascinated.

"It's not really that sensational. She's in the scene. But we were talking about your not doing any more videos where you get abused. I really don't like it."

"Okay, I'll do my best to avoid them," Teresa agreed with amusement.

"Anyway, Teresa, you should be spending less time on videos and sessions and more time on your art," he pointed out.

"You're right," she agreed again.

"I could help you by becoming your patron," Anthony suggested. "I've been thinking this out since I saw you."

"You like me that much?" Teresa had a pixie smile that Anthony adored.

"You know I've had a crush on you for years."

"But you live so far away," said Teresa wistfully.

"You'll just have to force yourself to visit New York once a month."

"But if you have a girlfriend in the scene, why do you need me?"

"Because Susan is a college girl and she's presently away at school having her own adventures."

"How old are you?"

"If you'd taken the trouble to glance at one of my albums you'd know that." he pretended to be offended.

"Actually my friend Paulie, who like most gay men, adores your music, told me that you're 41. I just wanted to see if you'd admit to it."

"Teresa, are you being fresh on purpose?"

"How old do you think I am?"

"Any man who answers such a question is a fool."

"I don't care. I'm 35. And you do have a huge gay following. They think you're gay."

"Teresa?"

"What?"

"You're one remark away from a spanking."

"If they knew what a pervert you are, they'd love you even more," she asserted.

Anthony took off his jacket and rolled up his sleeves, looking thoughtful. "Come over here, you," he took her by the arm, and taking a seat on the sofa facing the fireplace, pulled her across his lap. She disposed herself gracefully in this position, immediately pressing her flat mid section against his thighs and wriggling her hips in the adjustment.

"Calm down, Teresa."

"No!"

He smacked her hard.

"Ow!"

"Now tell me you haven't been gossiping about my perversions to half of West Hollywood."

"I haven't."

"Telling one is the same as telling all," he smacked her on the other cheek, without pulling her pants down.

"Ouch! I didn't tell anyone. I mean, Girlfriend at the OOTC party knew you before I did and told me who you were, so that doesn't count."

"It counts if you told her you were doing a session with me."

"Oh." Teresa hung her head.

"How do you think my suburban matinee ladies would feel about Anthony Newton if they knew he played B&D?"

"I swore Paulie to secrecy. And he practically worships you. When he found out how I insulted you the first night we met, he wanted to thrash me himself."

"And did he?" Anthony paused to pull down her leggings and reveal her sheer black panties, through which her white bottom gleamed.

"I suggested he bend me over the sofa arm and give me a good strapping to defend your honor, but he wasn't up to the challenge."

"Tell Paulie that he'll get an autographed album for every strapping he manages to give you this year. Now, who else have you told about us?" he slapped her hard through her panties.

"No one!"

"Are you sure, Teresa?" he pulled her panties down. Her bottom was already blushing. Now he held her fast and spanked her soundly, stopping at two dozen.

"I didn't know I wasn't supposed to tell anyone," she gasped when he stopped to rub.

"No? I always understood professionals to be respectful of confidentiality," Anthony chided her.

"I am respectful, but you have to tell me first if it's big deal," she defended herself weakly, trying desperately to remember whether she had told anyone else about Anthony Newton.

"Damn it, Teresa, of course it's a big deal with someone like me.

You should have known that," he scolded and resumed the spanking with a high degree of indignation. "You're lucky I'm just spanking you Teresa," he told her. "You really should have known better."

For Teresa, who lay across his knee with a palpitating heart, the line between playing and reality had become blurred. She tried to remember exactly what she had said to Paulie about Anthony and it suddenly filled her with horror. She'd told Paulie everything, including the dimensions of Anthony's penis.

"I'm so terribly sorry," she whimpered, steeling herself for more punishment. "How may I atone for my mistake?" she added, staying his hand with her eloquence.

"What would you suggest?" he asked, smoothing away the sting with his hand.

"I think that you should punish me severely," Teresa said with perfect trust.

"Would that teach you discretion?"

"I should hope so," she replied, turning back to look at him with soft brown eyes.

"Get me a hairbrush," he told her, folding his arms till her return. Teresa could not behold her urbane lover without a thrill, least of all when he struck such a pose, in his double-breasted wool cashmere suit. With the image of his charming demeanor imprinted on her mind, it was unbearably exciting to go back across his knee and feel her panties lowered for the hairbrush. She blessed her own good sense for bringing the lightest wooden hairbrush she owned on this trip.

Renewing his grip on her waist he raised his arm and said, "I never thought I'd have to school you in discretion, Teresa." He brought the brush down hard. It was a light brush, but its penetrating sting made her jump, squeak and put back her hand to rub.

"What's that hand?"

"I'm sorry."

"Move it if you please."

Teresa gingerly withdrew her hand and got another resounding smack with the back of the wooden brush. Then the strokes fell faster, with only a beat between each. The brush soon had her kicking her slim legs and gripping the sofa cushions for support.

"It pains me to have to do this," he told her, "but if you're going to be my protégée you're going to have to learn to be more circumspect."

"Yes, I see that now," agreed Teresa with all sincerity, timidly putting back one hand to rub. He took her wrist and moved her hand then returned to smacking her resoundingly on the bottom with the back of the hairbrush.

"I don't want to have to repeat this lesson," he lied, pausing to survey her bottom. A dark pink hue suffused her fair skin. "You're getting twelve of the best," he told her. Then the first smack fell.

"Ow! I'm sorry, Anthony, I'll never speak your name to a living soul again," she promised fervently.

"Or write it in your diary," he stipulated.

"I don't keep one."

"Thank goodness." The brush fell again and again she cried out.

"Please forgive me?" she put one hand back to rub her bottom, where a bright pink imprint had appeared to match the one he had already left on the other cheek.

"I do forgive you, but you still have to be punished." He smacked her twice more, hard enough to cause hot tears to spring to her eyes. She had seldom begun to cry so soon into a spanking, but she felt so humiliated by her own unguarded tongue that an emotional outburst seemed inevitable. In two more smacks she was sobbing aloud.

"Why, Teresa, tears from you? After only six with the hair brush?" Anthony lay the brush aside and lifted her from his lap. He handed her a handkerchief.

"I can take more," she protested.

"I'm sure you can but I got through to you, and that's all I wanted to do."

"I wish I hadn't been such a bad girl."

"You are my worst nightmare," he told her pleasantly. When this caused her to sigh with regret he told her he was teasing her and ravished her smooth white throat until she was assured of his abiding passion for her.

The week after Teresa went home Anthony was imbued with such warm and affectionate feelings for his new mistress that material acts of generosity soon followed. He set up an artistic endowment to furnish her with a substantial monthly stipend, obviating the need for Teresa to continue accepting uncomfortable sessions and unpleasant videos. He wished her to be solely dependent upon him for patronage, in order to free her from her economic enslavement to others.

She flew home on Wednesday and he had a letter from her by Saturday, filled with love, admiration and line art. She had a feeling when he handed her the envelope just before she got on the plane that happy multiples of Ben Franklin's benign countenance resided within it, but was never the less awed when she saw how many he had crowded in. She had thought his talk of patronage charming, but hadn't understood at all what he had meant. Now she knew he meant to keep her.

Meanwhile, it was Paige who was charged with carrying out Anthony's noble impulses, from Teresa's first class plane tickets to the white roses for her room. Paige thought at first that Miss Clifford was an actress being considered for one of Anthony's productions, but when she asked him if this was the case, he replied that Teresa was an artist in whom he had taken an interest and that this was not a subject to be discussed with Susan Ross. At this strict injunction Paige had blushed as dreadfully as he had ever seen her blush and fled in confusion to her office. After her fear at having offended him with her prying evaporated, it was quickly replaced by frustrated jealousy.

Having a solid selection of suitors in the scene had not deterred Paige from continuing to love and desire her boss. Suddenly being made aware of a rival, who was no doubt brilliant and glamorous as well as beautiful, plunged Paige into moments of black despair. She wondered whether even the delicious afternoon discipline sessions would come to an end because of this new young lady. But when she lifted her head from her desk and met her own smart, appealing new image in the carved oak mirror opposite, the effect was bracing.

The transformation, which Anthony's good taste and deep pockets had wrought, was remarkable, and Paige would forever regard him as the man who had rescued her youth for her. Even the eyeglasses he'd chosen seemed to enhance the sudden beauty of her face. Her fair skin held no lines, her slender form no imperfections. The good clothes he had bought her emphasized her trim waist and elegant thigh line.

"Just once in your life you could be daring," she told the mirror. "What's the worst he could do?" She knew he would never fire her for mere impertinence. So she waited for the proper moment, which was on the following Tuesday afternoon, in the middle of a snowstorm, when she knew that Anthony had no plans to leave the house at all.

She had formed a small plan, which she immediately put into effect. Slipping into the dressing room that adjoined her office, she exchanged her smart little Jones New York suit for a short, tight, shiny, black spandex tube dress, which she accessorized with 4" heels, dispensing all together with stockings and underwear. Then she sat at her desk with a violently thumping heart and waited for the inevitable moment when Anthony would stop into her office to chat. That moment came almost as soon as she sat down.

She started to blush immediately as the sight of her in the spandex dress froze him with amazement.

"Paige, what the hell are you wearing?"

"A dress," she responded.

"I fill your wardrobe with elegant clothes and you come to work in that? What's the matter with you, young lady?"

"Don't you like it?"

"I hate it more than I hate strip malls and pink frosted lipstick. Have you learned nothing from my sage fashion counsel? That dress is too short, too tight and too cheap even to wear to a biker bar no less to work in my house."

"Oh," Paige hung her head.

"Suppose some friends or associates stop by? They might think I actually encourage my secretary to dress like a slut."

"Really, Mr. Newton, if the dress bothers you that much, I don't have to wear it at all," said Paige, and with apparent indifference, stood up, unzipped her dress and let it drop to the floor, leaving her completely naked on high heels.

Rendered momentarily speechless by this defiant display of pure beauty, Anthony stared at her for a long moment. Paige O'Connor thinking up a prank as mischievous as this all on her own was a breakthrough that was the scene equivalent of Helen Keller surprising her teacher, Anne Sullivan, with her ability to use language.

"All right, young lady, what are you up to?" he finally demanded.

"My boss hates a dress, I hate it too," she replied pertly and sat down at her computer to return to work. Anthony had never seen a naked girl in high heels seated at her secretarial station before and he allowed himself to appreciate the image for several moments before calling her to order.

"I see," he did not seem to be amused by her impudence as he removed his suit jacket and dropped it on a chair. Loosening his tie and unbuttoning his collar, he went across the room and sat on the tufted leather chaise, lying back against it with one leg on the floor and the other stretched out. "Come over here," he ordered summarily, undoing more shirt buttons and fixing her with a cool glance that pierced her with pleasure and pain.

"Why?" she arose from her chair trembling, "What are you going to do?"

"Paige, don't make me ask you again."

She came to him at once. He held her eyes with his as he deliberately released his large, thick, erect penis from his grey flannel trousers and allowed it to nod in her direction. Paige had felt this noble engine of desire many times under her tummy while he had spanked her across his lap, but she had never seen it before and was duly impressed by its ample dimensions and apparent flexibility.

"Spread your legs," he told her when she came to him. While he held one hand firmly against her tummy, he slipped the middle finger of his other hand up into her vagina, and kept it there until she became sufficient wet to proceed. "I want you dripping wet before I fuck the living day lights out of you. Do you understand?"

"Yes, sir," she sighed with pleasure as he probed her skillfully

"You've got a lot of nerve pushing my buttons like that," he told her.

"I got your attention," she pointed out.

"You deserve a good spanking for that." He gently disengaged his hand and used it to brandish his cock at her. "I hate friction when I'm fucking. Get it wet." She immediately understood and went happily down on her knees to give him head. "Slow down, sweetie," he told her, stroking her hair, "I just want you to get it wet. That's enough. Now come over here and lie on top of me," he instructed, taking her in his arms. His cock lay between them, against her smooth belly. With one hand he held her about the waist, with the other, he massaged her bare bottom, encouraging her to grind against him. He squeezed, spanked and caressed her bottom until her clitoris throbbed with desire.

"Take me inside you," he told her, taking his cock in his hand and lightly positioning it against her creamy labia. She shyly but deftly reached down to ease his access into her snug, moist slit. He entered her painlessly in spite of his daunting size, and she took her hand away and allowed him to pull her against him again. Now he slipped up into her inch by ramrod inch, sending violent shivers of pleasure through her entire body as he achieved full penetration. She bent her knees to lock against his waist as he held her flawless bottom in both hands.

"You shouldn't have played such a naughty prank," he told her seriously, holding her firmly by the waist and raising his hand to slap her bottom. She sensed it coming and clung to him. His hand impacted against her cheek, driving her harder against him. "Say you're sorry," he recommended, spanking her bare bottom smartly.

"I'm sorry!" she hastened to reply.

"You've been unforgivably impertinent," he informed her, pausing to massage her bottom and thrust his cock deeper into her velvet recesses. "Forcing the issue of sex in the workplace is in such bad taste."

"I know," she admitted, then added, with great difficulty, "and I want to be punished."

Anthony took her at her word and applied the palm of his hand vigorously to her bottom while possessing her completely with his cock. Under the double assault she climaxed quickly. He waited to yield to his own desire until he had her on her knees and was in her to the hilt from behind. In this position he continued the spanking. She became aroused all over again and gave up another shuddering orgasm, which served as a catalyst to his. After which they all but fell asleep in each other's arms on the recamier, he almost fully dressed and she completely naked.

When Paige woke up Anthony was sitting in a chair looking at her.

"I'm far from satisfied with your behavior," he informed her.

"I'm sorry."

"Did I not stress to you that I already have a girlfriend?"

"But that doesn't stop you from seeing Miss Clifford," Paige shyly pointed out.

"Oh, so that's what this was about."

"It's just that when I realized you were keeping a mistress, I thought you might have changed your mind about being faithful to your girlfriend."

"First of all, I am not keeping a mistress and secondly, when I change my mind on any subject we've discussed, I'll let you know about it," he bristled with irritation, causing the high color of embarrassment to flood her cheeks. However, he immediately softened this injunction with a promise. "Paige, I don't want spoil our time together by disciplining you now, but tomorrow afternoon you're going to be properly punished for your presumption."

Because he was actually somewhat annoyed at the temerity of his secretary in forcing him to confront the perfection of her nude body, Anthony determined to give Paige six of the best with the cane, though he did not tell her that this was what to expect. This was probably just as well because he changed his mind that night during dinner out with non-scene friends, when he had plenty of time for inward reflection. She had certainly been charming, his pretty protégée, fitting against him so perfectly, and then coming so nicely for him. The caning became a strapping in his study. But that night, as he fell asleep watching the fire in his bedroom grate, he decided instead to punish her with greater intimacy, possibly right there in his own bedroom suite. "She is a dear little thing," he thought to himself, impulsively dialing her number.

Startled out of sleep to hear her phone ring at eleven thirty, Paige answered with the caution of someone used to receiving bad news.

"Oh, I'm sorry, honey. I didn't realize you turned in so early."

"Oh, Mr. Newton! It's all right," her voice betrayed wonder at being called by him at home. "But why are you calling?"

"Oh, just to warn you not to try any nonsense like calling in sick to avoid your punishment tomorrow," he said casually.

"Oh, Mr. Newton!" she replied with rich amusement.

"Why do you laugh?"

"Because you know why," she said.

"No, why?"

"Because I'm looking forward to it," she admitted.

"That's just because you've never been caned before. If you had, you'd be dreading it," he sagely informed her.

"I have too been caned. I was caned just the other night by a man I met through my ad."

"Well, in that case I'll just have to give you that strapping you never quite got in Hollywood, instead. I much prefer the strap to the cane anyway. One can use it longer and harder," his haughty tone excited her, though she knew that the point of this call was simply to find her in pleasant spirits after their time together.

"I much prefer the strap as well," she echoed him softly.

The following afternoon found Anthony in a romantic mood and he had Paige come up to his bedroom for her discipline. She was dressed in a cranberry red wool dress with a full skirt. When he lay her face down on the brocade counterpane and turned up her skirt to reveal her pristine underpinnings, it was not before placing two plump pillows under her mid section to elevate her adorable bottom. Anthony had always been susceptible to sheer white nylon panties and white lace garter belts, particularly in combination with beige stockings and black high heeled maryjanes. With her shiny chestnut pageboy and the portrait collar, drop waist dress, Paige possessed a winsome charm he'd not noticed before.

He had chosen to use a lightweight but effective tooled leather strap on her panty-clad seat. He sat beside her on the bed and stroked her bottom. "Do you know why you're being punished, Paige?" his tone was mild and seductive.

"Because I took off all my clothes?" she peeked over one shoulder.

"Are you taking this seriously?" he looked stern.

"Yes," she said, biting her lip.

"Then why do you look like you're about to giggle?" he demanded.

"I'm sorry," she dropped her eyes.

He got to his feet and picked up the strap. "Paige?"

"Yes, sir?"

"You deliberately took your clothes off in order to seduce me, did you not?"

"Yes," she sighed.

"When I've made it a point to tell you several times how imprudent I thought an office affair might be," he added in a tone of profound disappointment.

"I'm sorry," she repeated, more timidly still.

"I wonder what got into you," he brought the strap down smartly across her panties. She caught her breath and ground against the pillows under her tummy. Her fair bottom colored immediately through the sheer nylon. "What got into you, Paige?" The strap came down again.

"Mischief, I guess," she raised her head.

"Is that so?" he paused to lower her panties to her knees, then deliver two more smart strokes, now to her bare bottom. "Well, I'm sure that I enjoy a bit of mischief in a girl better than most men," he gave her blushing bottom a rub. "But not when that girl is also my employee." Two more smacks with the wide leather strap brought up the pink again. Soft whimpers issued from her childish red mouth, but she thrust her bottom up for the strap so invitingly that Anthony began to lay it on harder.

After a dozen or so strokes he lay the strap aside and smoothed her bottom with his hand.

"Oh, please!" she cried.

"What, sweetie?" he let his lips graze her punished bottom.

"Please don't spare me," she shyly said.

"No?"

"Remember how I got off so lightly in California?"

"Did you?" he smiled, remembering her bent over the marble table in that sun drenched suite.

"So you really owe me two strappings. Two hard ones," she suggested. Then she hid her face. She had said more than enough. Anthony was impressed. He took off his jacket, rolled up his sleeves and took up the strap again. Then he used it on his secretary's bare, upturned bottom until his arm got tired. She arched to it the entire time, though the strokes came hard and fast until well over a hundred had been given, staining her delicate skin a deep magenta.

Anthony had never given anyone that kind of strapping before. If it had been Susan on the receiving end, he would have called it unacceptably severe, but Paige appeared to be developing a high tolerance for corporal discipline, and it was obvious that she had an affinity for the strap.

Nonetheless, he stopped before she would have him do so, violently aroused by her passionate submission. As the strapping had progressed she had spread her thighs in goddess-like abandon and now her excitement glistened on her soft pubic curls. She was now up on her knees, in an exquisite posture for rear penetration. Nor could he deny himself this pleasure, in spite of all he had just said.

Taking her was the work of a moment, though he stretched the exercise to twenty minutes of deep insertion, with the last five being in her bottom. He'd begun with the pure intention of disciplining her into more sensible behavior and ended by sodomizing her. But how could one resist penetrating a bottom as pink as carnations and smooth as a peach?

Afterwards he felt terribly guilty. He handed her a cup of tea as she sat dreamily brushing her hair in an armchair by his bedroom fireside.

"It seems I've made a sad mess of keeping our relationship businesslike," he confessed, confused as to how to proceed. It now appeared that in spite of his best intentions, making love to her once had been as good a opening Pandora's box. Limiting the course of their play in this respect now seemed absurd. But where would or could it lead? Anthony was troubled. Paige, on the other hand, seemed almost merry.

"Mr. Newton, may I share a secret with you?"

"Paige," he bristled, "do you want a spanking on top of the

strapping, right now?"

"No," she faltered, reaching back to rub her very well strapped bottom.

"Then kindly don't call me Mr. Newton at a time like this. Now what's the secret?"

"Well, guess what I did last night?"

"I can't imagine." Anthony was intrigued by her sudden animation.

"I suppose it was awful and greedy of me, after having my dream come true of...of you making love to me, but I went out on a date."

"Oh?" he smiled encouragingly, impressed that she had the composure to actually arrange a second social event after accomplishing the daring office seduction.

"Yes. It was with a very nice man I'd seen before. He'd answered my ad and we've begun to date."

"In the scene?"

"Yes, completely. Especially strapping," she blushed. "My personal favorite."

"Great. I'm so proud of you, Paige!" Anthony's spirits soared as he observed her new independence.

"But you haven't heard the best part, Mr. Newton," she said with excitement.

"Paige! What did I tell you?"

"I mean Anthony," she stammered.

"Okay, you got through that. Now tell me the rest."

"Look!" Paige flashed a diamond ring at him. "He gave me this last night. We've become engaged. He's a handsome real estate lawyer with a beautiful home in Forest Hills. I'm going to be married, Mr. Newton. Me!" she hugged him with such intense happiness that he refrained from correcting her again.

"Paige, you amaze and delight me," he returned her embrace with exquisite relief.

"I could never have attracted the attention of a person like Melmond if it weren't for you, Mr. Newton."

"Melmond?"

"Of course Melmond must never know or guess just how much you've done for me," Paige cautioned timidly.

"Of course, dear girl. But you don't plan to leave me, I hope?"

"Oh, no sir! I want to work for you for as long as you'll have me!" replied the modest, sensible girl.

Anthony happily and gratefully drank his tea with a conscience newly cleansed and fresh for the next temptation.

Chapter Three

Chronicles of Random Point

For many months after he caned her, Laura Random made herself virtually inaccessible to Hugo Sands. This frustrated him, as he knew from lawyer Cooper, that Laura's divorce from William would be finalized shortly.

She came to his annual Halloween party, stunning in a black chiffon ball gown, and played with everyone but Hugo. Then she and Marguerite Alexander left for Europe for six weeks.

Laura returned to Random Point in mid-December without bothering to visit Hugo's shop for Christmas gifts. When they met by chance in the village, a brief, bland "How are you?" was all he received from Laura, who then refused to look at him until he walked away.

Laura knew that she was meant to belong to Hugo Sands. But she had an instinct not to make it easy for him. She forgave him for the caning fairly quickly, but the embarrassment of the public humiliation remained a strong memory. She felt unable to confront him for months, not knowing what her attitude ought to be.

Then, one day in the Summer, as Laura Random drank her morning coffee on a balcony of Anthony Newton's house, she finally changed her point of view. It was a deep blue morning, the sea air smelled sweet and she felt restless with longing for a man who understood her needs.

She bathed and dressed in a linen halter dress and ankle strap sandals and made a ponytail out of her long, chestnut brown hair. She placed three color illustrations mounted and covered with tissue in her large leather portfolio and left the house. Laura drove down the hill and into the village; parking her old Thunderbird in front of Hugo Sand's antiques shop.

No one was in the main room when she entered, so she freshened her dark red lipstick in one of the many mirrors. At the tinkle of the bell Hugo came out of his office in back and was agreeably surprised to see Laura so bright, fresh and smiling before him.

"Why, Laura, how nice to see you," he said, coming around from behind the counter and taking the liberty of kissing her on the cheek. She allowed this without returning the embrace and slipped lightly out of his reach immediately.

"Do you have a few minutes?" she asked in a blandly friendly tone.

"Sure. All the time you want."

"Can we go in your office? I brought something to show you," she preceded him. Once they were in Hugo's office she opened the portfolio.

"Here are some drawings I've been working on for you. I hope you can use them," she said, displaying her work.

"They're beautiful, Laura. Of course I can use them. I can write you a check right now if you like."

"That won't be necessary. I'll send you an invoice."

"Fine," Hugo said, studying the exquisite pieces in detail.

"I did have another reason for coming by," she said, pulling a large manila envelope out of the portfolio.

"Oh?" he sat on the edge of his desk.

"I have an ad that I'd like you to put into your next issue."

"An ad?"

"A personal ad. With a photo," she pulled an 8"x 10" glossy out of the envelope; a studio portrait of herself in a leather dress that showed every slender curve of her beautifully proportioned body. Her smile was naughty. Hugo looked over her ad, which read,

"Submissive female, 30, professional illustrator, seeks attractive, non-pompous dominant for playmate. Send photo, letter and phone to:

Laura R., c/o New Rod magazine"

Hugo looked at her.

"You're placing an ad?"

"Yes."

"For a dominant?"

"Yes."

"You don't reveal much about yourself."

"The photo should get the job done," she said.

"Yes," Hugo agreed disagreeably.

"What's the matter?" she asked.

"The bit about non-pompous dominant. Is that intended for me?" he asked.

"Why would it be?" she parried.

He threw the ad and photo down on his desk, folded his arms and looked at her in a way that made her uncomfortable.

"Have I said something to upset you?" she asked innocently. "Now I hardly dare bring up the other item I wished to discuss."

"Go ahead, live dangerously," he encouraged her.

"Very well," she brought out yet another manila envelope with another ad and photo of herself. In this one she was voluptuously attired in a richly figured silk-satin brocade Victorian corset with her bottom and bosom exposed. Draped across an ottoman, Laura looked into the camera and invited the viewer to have his way with her. "I was wondering if you had room to run this ad as well in your pro section." She handed it to Hugo who looked it over briefly.

"Laura, this photo is much too sexy. You should know better," he told her sternly, becoming more annoyed by the moment.

"Hugo, whatever do you mean? You've shown nudity before."

"Not in a pro ad. It isn't dignified. All right, let me read the ad." Hugo glanced at her pro ad with a critical eye.

"Intelligent submissive available by appointment for B&D, role playing and moderate corporal punishment fantasies. Send photo, phone and letter to: Laura Rose c/o this magazine." He pondered this a moment.

"I'd say run one or the other ad but not both," he told her objectively.

"Really?'

"Run the pro ad but use the classy leather dress photo instead of the slave kitten one," he advised.

"Why not run both?"

"Because no one will pay you if they think you're available the other way."

"H'm," she said thoughtfully.

"Are you doing it for the money or for kicks?"

"Oh, both," she said casually, studying the photos.

"Didn't you get some sort of settlement from William?"

"No."

"Why not?"

"Oh, I spent enough of his money while we were married."

"Laura, you've been very foolish. You should have gotten a settlement," he scolded.

Laura shrugged and smiled. "He'll bail me out if I ever need it. I'm not worried."

"The point is, you really shouldn't be doing sessions," he said, as if suddenly coming to his senses.

"Why ever not?"

"Because you're not cut out for it. For every so-called moderate session you arrange there will be a severe one you'll hate. I really have to counsel you to drop this whole idea," he firmly told her.

"The money I get for my illustrations barely pays for my dry cleaning."

"What have you been doing up until now?"

"I had some money from William to start with, but now that's gone. Since I'm living in Anthony's house I don't have to worry about rent and the car is paid for. But I still have personal expenses. Not enough to warrant getting a full time job but enough that I need one additional source of income."

Hugo lit a cigarette while trying to decide which ad to run for Laura. The personal ad was more likely to produce serious rivals for Hugo than the pro one. But the pro ad was more likely to land Laura in unlucky situations.

"What did you do before you met William?"

"I was a commercial artist in a small Boston ad company. I made thirteen dollars an hour. I shared expenses with my then-boyfriend, with whom I lived. Of course, before I met William, I had less expensive tastes."

"Look, Laura, I have an idea. Why don't you forget this session scheme and let me help you out for awhile?" he tried to sound casual but couldn't help revealing some emotion as he made the offer he'd been planning to make to Laura since the first day they'd met.

"Thanks, but that sounds a lot scarier than sessions," she declined politely, causing the color to flood his face.

"Would you care to explain that remarkable statement?" Hugo's tone was icy.

"I'm not a slave," she said bluntly.

"Who said you were?"

"But you're a Master. Therefore, whoever you take for a mistress must necessarily become your slave."

"Laura, I've never regarded you as a slave or wanted you to be one. Rather, I've thought of you as my protégée."

"Call it what you will, you're too strict for me," Laura came to the point with a deep blush. This problem with Hugo had perplexed her for months.

Upon hearing this pronouncement Hugo relaxed somewhat.

"Laura, don't tell me you're still sulking about the caning."

"I'm not sulking. It's merely that the incident elucidated a facet of your character of which I had been previously unaware," Laura carefully replied.

"You had a serious attitude problem that month that I felt it needed correcting."

"Not that hard, it didn't," she protested, remembering the incident with fresh resentment.

"Laura, you're a spoiled brat. Didn't you realize that now and then you have to pay your dues?"

"I don't know what you mean."

"Don't you? You know, you've never really been properly grateful to me for discovering you. But if you think about it, you, who once toiled for $13 an hour, now lead a life of luxury and ease because one day four years ago I put your photo and illustrations in my magazine."

Laura stared out his office window at the duck pond across the street and remembered the utter monotony of her life before discovering the scene. Hugo was absolutely right; everything had changed within weeks of first writing to the erudite publisher.

"Yes, Laura," he continued, warming to his subject, as he saw the guilty flush steal across her cheek, "I even got you an affluent husband, as well as a wealthy brother-in-law to-be, in whose home you now reside. In fact, speaking of Anthony Newton, let's not forget what I did for your little sister Susan in introducing the two of them, an introduction from which you now benefit immensely as well. But are you grateful for any of this?"

"I am grateful," she said, suddenly feeling guilty. "I'm sorry, Hugo. You're right. You have changed my life. I didn't realize that I'd never even thanked you for that." she added.

"I shouldn't have to remind you of that."

"I'm sorry," she murmured.

"Now what in the world was in your head when you came over here today?" he demanded. Laura's lips trembled and she hid her face.

"I have to go," she suddenly said and bolted for the door. He interposed himself between her and it and forced her to look at him. Sure enough, he had put tears in her eyes.

"You're not going anywhere until we clear up a few things between us," he told her, leading her to a chair where he made her sit down. "Why are you crying?" She dashed her tears away and shook her head. "I'll tell you why you came over today, Laura." he paced. She said nothing. "You know damn well that you don't need to place an ad. You have enough connections by now to get plenty of boyfriends in the scene without that. This whole interview has simply been a personal bid for attention from me. Hasn't it?"

Laura wasn't prepared to agree to this and rose to leave once more.

"I'll let you go now," Hugo said, "but I want you to think about what I've said and call me later."

Laura didn't get into her car when she left the antique shop but strolled across the street to the duck pond and sat on a bench for some time, thinking about what Hugo had said and how handsome he had looked and how stern.

Hugo watched her from his office window, moodily smoking and mentally excoriating himself for allowing her to slip through his fingers again. The fact that she was not immediately leaving the neighborhood was encouraging though. Suddenly she got up and began to walk slowly back to the shop, her heart thrilling to the flowery scent of the warm wind that wafted through Random Point that afternoon.

This time Laura had to wait until several customers had browsed and left before being able to speak to Hugo. When they were alone she went up to the counter. The clocks in the shop began to toll the hour of four.

"I thought about what you said," she began.

"And?" Hugo's heart was pounding as violently as Laura's, though his outward demeanor was cool.

"And I have to admit I came over here looking for trouble today."

"That's what bad girls do. I should turn you over my knee."

A spasm rippled through her tummy as Hugo came around from behind the counter, took Laura by her bare forearm and pulled her through the narrow aisles of antique bric-a-brac which lined the shop until they arrived at a tall, mirrored valet furnished with an upholstered seat. Hugo sat down and pulled Laura down across his lap, though very carefully because of the many breakables surrounding them.

"Hugo, no! What if someone comes in!"

"I don't care," he said, positioning her properly and raising his hand. Her simple linen sheath dress hugged the contours of her slim buttocks snugly. He spanked her soundly several dozen times on the seat of her skirt. The feel of his hand on her bottom was warm and sharp. She kicked a bit and cried, "Oh!" whenever a harder smack fell.

"So you came over today to start trouble, did you? With your impertinent ads and insulting witticisms!" he pulled up her skirt carefully. "Lift up," he ordered, completing the act and exposing her lace edged white silk panties and slim bare legs.

"I didn't insult you," she protested, looking back at him.

"No?" he rested both forearms on the small of her back and leaned down to look at her. "Then what was that stuff about feeling safer doing sessions with strangers than becoming my lover?"

"That was because you...scared me that time."

"You mean when I caned you? I didn't scare you, Laura. You scared yourself. For once you were truly submissive. You held still for something you didn't like."

"But it upset me. It didn't feel right. And if I become your girlfriend, you'll make me do that all the time!" she replied.

"Oh, I will not," he said, with irritation. "I don't know how you can say that when I've hardly ever spanked you harder than I would a twelve year old. That's what I mean about insulting." To drive this point home Hugo warmed Laura's panties thoroughly with the palm of his hand. It came down hard and rhythmically, with the skip of a beat between smacks until the entire surface of her bottom seemed to radiate heat between skin and silk.

"I'm tired of waiting whole seasons to see you," Hugo paused to pull her panties down and bare her pinkened bottom. "Do you understand?" A smack caused her to whimper her assent.

"Yes!"

Hugo administered a long, fairly hard spanking to Laura. He had spanked many women in his forty-seven years but Laura was his favorite. He held her tightly around her slender waist all the while he spanked her and was pleasantly conscious of her weight across his thighs. Then thinking of the many months he'd had to do without her, he spanked her harder.

Laura ceased to struggle. It had been a long time since she'd had a really sound spanking and Hugo's indignation heightened her excitement. She could feel a difference in the way he held her today, as though he really cared. She didn't mind if the spanking went on, so long as he held her like that.

Hugo paused to rub her bottom and scold her.

"From now on, Laura, we're not going to have any misunderstandings. I've been in love with you for years and it's time you became mine." He continued to caress her while she ground against his lap. "And I don't want to hear any nonsense about you being afraid of me. You know damn well you can wrap me around your little finger any time you want. Don't you?" he smacked her hard.

"Yes," she replied quickly and honestly.

"Well? You know that we were meant to be together. What do you have to say?" he stayed his hand again and squeezed her punished flesh.

"I say okay," she replied, embarrassed at discussing such a topic while in this position. Hugo pulled her up to sit on his lap.

"You say okay?" he kissed her lightly on the lips.

"Yes, that will be fine," she looked back at her reddened bottom and gave it a rub. He hugged her to him and kissed the perfumed places between her throat and ears until she squirmed against him.

"And you will not do any sessions," he told her sternly, "or place any personal ads. And if you fuck anyone else you'd better not let me find out about it. I'm establishing a new order as of today." He made her stand up and he did too. Laura pulled her panties back and her skirt back down, arguing with nothing.

"Fancy a Bennington girl having to recourse to sessions for her living," said Hugo with cutting accuracy. "You ought to follow Marguerite's example. She already owns a house and a shop and she was only one year ahead of you in school. And look at your friend Patricia Fairservis. She's got an excellent position and the respect of her colleagues. And neither of them is any smarter than you. You managed to show some pluck while William was out of town by running his company, but the instant he returned, you reverted to your idle, self-indulgent ways. Would you tell me, Laura Random, what you've been doing for the past nine months? I mean besides the three drawings."

Laura looked uncomfortable.

"It's time for a change, my dear," he told her firmly. "I'm going to design a production schedule for you that if consistently followed will result in your producing a hundred page graphic novel by Christmas."

Laura looked at him in surprise.

"And if you don't, you know what bad girls get."

Laura looked at him, then went to him and put her arms around his neck. He softened and embraced her.

"I have missed you," she murmured.

Chapter Four

Jealousy

Michael Flagg felt pleasantly excited yet profoundly uneasy about attending the first meeting of Pandora, the new B&D support group on Cape Cod. But this was only because every woman he had slept with for the past four years was going to be there, including his current sweetheart, Patricia Fairservis.

The orientation was given by the tall, sandy haired Hugo Sands, natty in a light linen suit, and the statuesque Marguerite Alexander, who showed spectacularly in a dress of black silk cobwebs. Hugo was in the midst of defining scene terminology when he was disturbed by the sound of Patricia whispering to her friend, Laura Random, encased in a snug, PVC apron dress.

Patricia was excited because she recognized the musical composer Anthony Newton sitting with Laura's little sister Susan Ross. "Goody! I finally get to meet him!" Patricia commented in a fairly audible tone to Laura, as magazine spreads of Newton's lavish homes unfolded in her mind.

Hugo looked directly at Patricia, who instantly subsided in her chair, having already been caned by Hugo on one occasion and recognizing that certain look in his eyes.

"Have you something to contribute, Patricia?" he asked her, in a tone that put everyone in mind of their most intimidating grade school teacher.

"No," she replied, blushing.

"Disturb this meeting once more and you'll be part of the corporal punishment demonstration," he warned her. Patricia bit her lip and began to nonchalantly study her fellow fetishists.

William Random, whose chiseled muscularity was revealed by pegged Levi's and a rolled sleeved white shirt, locked his arms around the waist of Michael's ex-wife Damaris in a manner that indicated a solid attachment.

"My god, you left that Calvin Klein ad for craggy old Hugo Sands?" Patricia queried Laura in a barely audible whisper. Yet, when she looked up she noticed with a start that Hugo was once again provoked by the interruption. Michael smiled behind his program while everyone else stared at Patricia. Especially Michael's ex-fiancée, Jane Eliot, who was extremely curious about the woman Michael had taken up with.

During the intermission, Jane was the first to come up to them, which was exactly when Patricia noticed that the lithe brunette was wearing the same halter dress from North Beach Leather she had on. A violent color flooded Patricia's face as she remembered that Michael had picked this one of the hundred dresses in her wardrobe.

"I was amazed when I saw your name on the program," Michael told Jane, after a friendly embrace and introductions.

"You'll never believe it, but I'm living with a woman now too," Jane confided unselfconsciously. "A bisexual woman," she added, indicating a tall, lean, blonde girl dressed in black jeans and a t-shirt, drinking beer across the room and talking to Hugo Sands and William Random.

"You and Marnie Price?" Michael recognized the wealthiest young woman in Random Point.

Jane now turned to Patricia with interest. "Obviously, we share the same taste in a couple of things," Jane said, regarding the dress on Patricia. "I hope it looks as good on me as it does on you," she added in her pleasant, non-threatening way. Patricia merely smiled in return, having not yet decided what her attitude towards Jane should be. She did not like the way Michael was smiling at Jane and eyeing Jane in the body sculpting dress.

"I just can't get over the fact that you feel comfortable enough with this stuff to actually lecture on the use of vibrators," Michael remarked, with an open admiration, which annoyed Patricia.

"I was such a pill when you knew me. I don't blame you for not attempting to enlighten me. I probably would have advised you to seek counseling."

"Instantly," he agreed.

"Well, everyone isn't equally gifted with an understanding of their own sexuality. Some of us need a guide. Hugo was the one who brought me out."

"Really? I know Hugo," said Patricia, suddenly more interested in Jane. Now it seemed they had shared two men in common! That almost made her more of a sister than a rival.

"But recently," Jane went on to explain, "I realized I could better integrate my new affinity for bondage and discipline with my ardent feminism by experiencing the scene with other women."

Patricia noticed Marnie Price eyeing her lover jealously from across this room and this reassured her.

"How did you two meet?" Jane asked.

"After Damaris left me I placed an ad. Patricia responded to it. She's married but her husband isn't in the scene." Michael revealed. Meanwhile, Patricia had almost lost interest in Jane, whose newfound lesbianism seemed to eliminate her as a rival.

Michael couldn't fail to notice Patricia staring across the room at his ex-wife, Damaris, who had joined William, Hugo and Marnie in conversation. Damaris was tightly corseted under her full-skirted, cranberry cocktail dress. Her chin-length hair was black and geometrically cut. Her face was open and untroubled, with big, dark eyes and a wide, beautiful mouth. William reflexively slipped his arm around her 23" waist as she stepped into the circle. Her bosom and bottom were well rounded and womanly.

Damaris had peeked over at Patricia and Michael at least once, and of course Patricia had noticed and it had chilled her. Damaris had given a little friendly smile and a very tiny wave, to indicate that she knew whom Patricia was and was prepared to be gentle about her replacement. Patricia managed a weak smile back and ran outside to smoke.

Outside the meeting hall, Susan Ross and her college friend, Diana Stratton, admired the row of motorcycles parked at the curb.

"Is the dick-of-death-detective here?" Diana begged Susan to tell her.

"Yes," replied Susan, who was 21, with long, wavy, goldenrod hair. Diana was 20, with a chestnut pageboy. Both were petite. Susan wore an a-line denim dress and Diana a navy gingham halter dress with a full skirt over a white petticoat. These little outfits were drawing attention away from the leather and latex ensembles, which clad the many svelte and voluptuous female forms now emerging from the hall into the balmy night air, but the girls remained oblivious of the stir they were creating as they lingered on the pavement, near the bikes.

"That's Michael's girlfriend over there," Susan explained, indicating Patricia, "I've only met her once. I think she's the jealous type and I'm sure she doesn't know I've played with him. So don't blurt out anything inappropriate," she added.

Just as Susan said this the girls saw Hugo stroll out of the hall and pause on the front porch for a moment to light a cigarette, but when he looked up and saw Patricia smoking at the curb he threw his away and strode over to her with a purposeful look which caused her to tingle with apprehension.

"What?" she challenged, with a hostile flare to her nostrils.

"What do you think?" he asked quietly.

"Hugo, you're not spanking me in public!" she declared.

"No?" Hugo took Patricia by the earlobe, as though she were an Edwardian schoolchild and using the bumper of Anthony Newton's Bentley as a bench, turned the willowy blonde over his knee. Patricia was so shocked that she could barely speak to protest as a small circle of amused on-lookers watched Hugo bring his palm down hard on the seat of her leather dress a dozen times.

"Chairing a meeting is hard enough without having to deal with rude girls talking out of turn," said Hugo, administering another twelve forceful smacks to Patricia's well-protected bottom before letting the furious girl up.

"Wow!" said Diana to Susan, "I think I'm in love."

"With which one?"

"You're right," said Diana, longing to put her arms around the stunning blonde woman and comfort her, yet even more violently drawn to the stern Pandora coordinator.

"How dare you?" Patricia cried, as he let her up. At that moment Michael stepped up to witness the end of the confrontation.

"Excuse me," Patricia said haughtily, and then strode back to the meeting hall. She had never felt so ill-used. It almost made her wish to seek revenge on Hugo Sands. She could easily undo all the good she had ever done him with one indifferent squib on his shop in her magazine. How dare he spank her in front of those two college girls, tattooed bikers and even Marguerite Alexander!

In the bathroom she lit another cigarette and swallowed a sob of anger. Laura immediately followed her in. She was Hugo's girlfriend now as well as Patricia's only female friend in the scene.

"Hey, what happened?" she scrutinized Patricia's face. "Are you upset? I heard Hugo spanked you."

"Yes, in front of twenty people. Including your sister and her friend. I thought I'd die."

"I wish I hadn't missed that!" Laura lamented rather heartlessly.

"Laura, he can't do things like that. Wasn't he just talking about consensual B&D? I didn't consent to play just now in front of two dozen people."

"You do have a point."

"How dare he lay hands on me in front of strangers? I hope Michael punched him out," Patricia folded her arms in glee at this thought.

"I guarantee that he didn't," Laura smiled.

"How can you deal with a man like that?" Patricia asked her, with a shiver.

"Diplomatically, I suppose."

"You mean you can never tell Hugo off? Because he's so fucking dominant?"

"You make a habit of telling Michael off?"

"No. But he doesn't need it."

"Well, at any rate, come on out so people won't think this was any big deal."

"All right, but Hugo had better apologize to me."

"Hugo never apologizes."

"Is that so? Well, Hugo Sands may soon find out that there are other forms of retribution besides physical!" Patricia threw down the dark glasses in disgust and savagely did her lipstick. Laura took a brush out of Patricia's purse and began to brush her friend's fine, blonde hair. Then Laura put the brush down and put her arms around Patricia's waist from behind. They looked at each other in the mirror and smiled.

"With that tiny little waist and gorgeous bottom, no wonder you get spanked so much," said Laura, kissing Patricia behind the ear. Patricia shivered and ground back against Laura.

Being the bad girls they were, Susan and Diana decided to cut the demonstration portion of the meeting and walk down to the edge of the village, where the water met the rocks, to smoke and discuss what they had already observed. Hugo Sands fascinated Diana.

"He was the first man to ever spank me," Susan told her friend as they tossed pebbles into the inky water. "He's always been in love with my sister. Now he's finally got her. But I don't think she can handle him."

"What do you mean?"

"Well, you saw how he acted tonight. He did something similar to me last year. In fact, he picked one night to humiliate both me and Laura in front of several people who are here tonight."

"What did he do?" Diana loved the idea of being punished publicly, especially by one so cool and composed,

"He spanked me for interrupting the grown-ups, much in the same way he just did to Patricia. Then he caned the hell out of Laura."

"Ooooh!" Diana shivered with excitement. "I wish he'd do that to me."

"No, you ridiculous girl, the way he caned my sister was excessive," Susan was surprised by her own vehemence in retrospect. "I ran and got William and he broke it up. Anthony was no help. He was enjoying the show. It took me a while to get over that."

"Hugo sounds delicious," said Diana. "Is he also the master of that ravishing redhead who's co-chairing?"

"Marguerite was a protégée of his at one time. She and my sister were at Bennington together."

"Whom does Marguerite belong to now?"

"Well, she's been quietly in love with Michael Flagg for years, but I think he's only one of several."

"I think Sherman Cooper is falling in love with me," Diana wisely concluded, enraptured by the moon.

"Have you done it yet?"

"No, but tonight I may allow it."

"Do you love him?"

"How could I not? We're the quintessential F. Scott Fitzgerald couple, he the Princeton bred lawyer, me the perverse, Vassar girl who's driving him insane. I hope we don't crash and burn."

When the meeting resumed, Marguerite Alexander gave a talk on restraints, demonstrating some simple rope ties on Laura Random. Next, Marguerite discussed the art of Victorian corseting, using as a subject the exquisite Damaris Flagg, who had removed her dress to reveal a black satin waist cinch, tightly laced. Her voluptuous bosom was enclosed in a black lace brassiere, but her round bottom was bare from mid-hip to thigh, the g-string affording her no modesty. Her beautifully turned legs were hosed in sheer black stockings, held up by the eight suspenders. Patricia could not take her eyes off the delectable creature who allowed Marguerite to fondle her slim hips and press her tiny waist in describing the virtues of corseting. How and why could Michael have abandoned this Venus? Patricia looked at her man with perplexity.

Marguerite filled Patricia with a greater fear. For as soon as she was brought to meet her, Patricia detected the faint, light perfume, which she sometimes smelled in Michael's wardrobe. This confirmed Marguerite as The Other One. Tall and striking, with the body of a showgirl and glasses, this independent woman was about Patricia's age, with a similar education and sophisticated taste. "The only difference between us is that I'm married and have smaller curves," thought Patricia gloomily.

Throughout the rest of the exhibitions, on piercing, latex, tattoos, transvestites and foot slaves, Patricia studied her various rivals. Then she caught Sherman Cooper looking at her and a new idea fluttered her heart. Perhaps she was foolish to spend her time worrying about other women when she might instead be flirting with other men!

After the demonstrations were concluded, almost everyone signed up to join as members in the new group. Then Anthony Newton told Hugo and Marguerite to invite anyone they liked to his house in Random Point for a party. He sent Laura back to open the house and alert Dennis that guests would shortly follow. Meanwhile, he and Sherman went to comb the town for Susan and Diana.

Patricia was talking to architect William Random, to whom she had just been introduced, about doing a story on him for the magazine, when she noticed Hugo gazing at her thoughtfully.

"You know, I'm thinking of buying a cottage on the Cape," Patricia told William, ignoring Hugo, "perhaps you could put me onto something good. I know you re-did Michael's place and I'm in love with it."

"I'll build you a house from scratch if you like," William said obligingly.

"I couldn't afford that."

"I own a construction company, so I can build at a very low cost. And the publicity of doing a house for Patricia Fairservis would be worth a special effort."

"You're very nice," smiled Patricia, still wondering why Laura had abandoned this beautiful, boyish young man for the distinguished yet somewhat faded Hugo Sands. Patricia, who had once admired Hugo's looks and style, could find nothing to appreciate about him that evening. She would, in fact, hate him till the day he died, she decided, turning from William to confront Hugo, who had crossed the room to stand at her elbow.

Patricia glared at him, pausing to frame a devastating set down when he astonished everyone within earshot by apologizing to her.

"Patricia, I wanted to say that I'm sorry I lost my temper with you earlier. It was totally out of line and if there's anything I can say or do to make it up to you, please tell me what it is," Hugo said with perfect sincerity. William was a witness to the seriousness with which the apology was made and was able to report on the confrontation faithfully later that night to the two or three people who asked him to confirm the event.

"Anything you can say or do, huh? You're lucky I'm not a switch," Patricia said, putting out her hand to shake his, adding, "Apology accepted." Hugo took her hand and kissed it rather nicely, thanked her and walked away.

"I wouldn't have believed that if I didn't see it," William said to Patricia, who couldn't suppress a small smirk of satisfaction herself.

"Oh, he probably overheard me say I'm moving to Random Point and wants to me to furnish my house though his shop," Patricia observed cynically.

Though in truth, it was more a matter of conscience than greed, which had prompted Hugo to apologize to a lady who had never done anything but good to him in their brief relationship. Her generous spreads on his shop had greatly increased his business the previous quarter and all he'd ever given her in return was a couple of hard corporal punishment sessions which had ended with her submissively on her knees and ready to serve him. It was true that in many ways she was an impossible princess, but she was not his princess and therefore he had no right to take her in hand. Besides, he hadn't enjoyed the look of disapproval on Susan's face when he let Patricia up. Susan and her sister Laura represented the modern reform movement in the scene, compliant to a point, yet instinctively rebellious against the clumsier aspects of male chauvinism in practice. Since Laura was his hard won girlfriend and Susan was her sister, it mattered to Hugo how both girls perceived his behavior. It was the nicety of their discernment that made the sisters so rare. An abject submissive was the easiest creature in the world to enthrall, an analytical one the most elusive. Laura had forced him to court her for years before accepting him as her dominant, thus he valued her above any other submissive he had ever loved.

Having discharged this duty, Hugo felt better and not at all compromised. Patricia softened as she watched him walk away. The fact that he had chosen to restore her dignity in front of another dominant male meant something to her. Perhaps he wasn't as much of a nightmare as she'd supposed. Tomorrow she would visit his shop and demand a present!

Diana had correctly identified the affliction of Sherman Cooper, who was now amusing Anthony Newton with his anxieties about the girls. Diana had made sure to let Sherman hear her invite Susan outside to admire the handsome Harleys.

"Perhaps some leather dykes will kidnap us and take by us force in the woods!"

Sherman was disturbed at the voicing of such dangerous wishes, though Anthony assured him that Diana had only said this to tease him. Sherman did worry about Diana constantly, because she was a thrill seeker. She would brag to him of her sexual adventures, to cause him to punish her harshly whenever they met. After he'd spanked her, she'd confess that she'd made the stories up. Sherman didn't know what to believe.

He adored Diana and felt that fate had finally provided him with The One. Hadn't she let him strap her the first day they met?

"I must be mad," Sherman confided to Anthony as they walked through the quiet town towards the shore, "becoming attached to a 20 year old!"

"She's a heart breaker all right," Anthony agreed, not very helpfully.

"You wouldn't believe the things she's told me she's done or wants to do," Sherman said, with active worry. "And she's a profoundly bad influence on Susan as well."

"Oh, I agree. Diana is a catalyst for trouble."

The men ran into the girls walking back through the village. Sherman did not say a word to Diana, to signify his displeasure about her abandoning the meeting. He now felt foolish about being an alarmist, seeing as the girls were just strolling along, but at the same time he was angry with Diana. It was hard to know what she wanted or expected from him. She had specifically invited him for the weekend, but now that he was here, she was virtually ignoring him.

The four times he'd seen her since their first meeting with Susan, had been perfect little scene dates, each including a dinner or lunch, a diversion such as a gallery, play or concert and a brisk corporal punishment session, generally based on the degree of mischief performed by Diana during the entertainment. It was usually something cute, like attempting to unzip his trousers under their coats during a performance of Hedda Gabler. But tonight there were many other dominants available to fuss over Diana, so he wondered why she should need him here at all.

When it was time to get into the Bentley, Diana got in front, with Anthony behind the wheel and left Susan to sit in back with Sherman, who was distinctly brooding.

"What the matter, Sherman?" Susan squeezed his hand and rubbed the back of it against her soft cheek.

"Is Diana deliberately trying to provoke me?"

"I don't know about that but I think she likes you very much," Susan informed him.

"She has an odd way of showing it," Sherman pointed out.

"She's a brat. As a friend I'd advise you to thrash her," Susan said. "Really make her cry. That's what she's waiting for."

"But I don't want to make her cry," Sherman protested.

"Oh, come on, every dominant wants to make his girlfriend cry at least once."

"Well, I certainly don't and I wouldn't presume to call Diana my girlfriend."

"She could be, you know. But you have to scare the hell out of her to make her respect you. Otherwise, she'll walk all over you. She'll make you her submissive. I can see the indications."

Since Susan was Diana's best friend and confidante, Sherman considered what she told him very seriously. However, it was difficult to adapt his own personal notions of chivalry to the needs of an insatiable and decadent young girl.

Susan Ross didn't feel that she was counseling her dear friend Sherman improperly since she herself had worn out her arm in spanking Diana without hearing a single plea for mercy.

When they reached Anthony's house on the cliff-side road overlooking Random Point, Diana immediately abandoned the entire group to go and search for Marguerite Alexander. She had played with several older women, but they had been older pro doms from the city and the scenes had had a maternal feel to them, which Diana didn't crave. Marguerite was just old enough to be worldly and wise, but still young enough to be dashing, a model to aspire to, and a goddess to submit to. She had heard from Susan that Marguerite was an expert whip mistress and she had longed to be whipped while lashed to a whipping post, for as long as she could remember. Marguerite was able to gratify this quaint ambition within moments of their introduction at the impromptu champagne bar, which Dennis had set up. They went directly up to the small ballroom, which Anthony was transforming, into an airy dungeon. There they found several couples that had been at the Pandora meeting already playing, but the whipping post was unoccupied.

When Sherman wandered into the room a few minutes later he was treated to the sight of the tall, russet-haired Marguerite whipping the bare buttocks of the girl he adored. Diana's arms were fastened around the carved, light mahogany whipping post. The skirt of her dress as well as her white crinoline had been tucked up above her waist and her white silk panties had been pulled down to her knees. By this time, her fair skin had been marked by the whip with many lashes, so that a dark pink hue suffused the entire surface of her dainty bottom. Sherman was depressed to note that the same delightful pants and groans Diana breathed while he played with her, could be extracted just as readily from his darling by Marguerite Alexander. He had no doubt, now that he thought of it, that anyone might be able to elicit a similar response from Diana, if only they knew enough to whip her.

Michael and Patricia sat on a love seat and watched the whipping of Diana with rapt attention. Her love of beauty and eroticism permitting her to forget that Marguerite was her archrival, Patricia admired wholeheartedly the perfection with which the voluptuous redhead was teasing and tormenting her enchanting captive. Marguerite was currently using an antique riding crop to separate Diana's legs and touch up her parted bottom cheeks. But sometimes Marguerite would stop punishing Diana all together and simply make her ride the crop.

"Why don't you offer to take her place, Patricia?" Michael suggested.

"I'm sure you would you enjoy that." Patricia replied.

"I feel cheated that I didn't get to see your first public spanking," said Michael, referring to the brief spectacle that Hugo Sands had made of her outside the meeting hall.

"I don't mind showing off, but I won't be whipped by anyone but you," she surprised him by replying.

No one had ever seen Michael Flagg play in public before, except for the one time Marguerite and half dozen customers in her bookshop watched Michael give Laura Random a birthday spanking several years before. So it was with a great deal of interest that such personages as Susan Ross, Damaris Flagg, Jane Eliot and Marguerite Alexander observed Michael leading his glamorous blonde companion to the whipping post when Diana had been freed from it. He removed his jacket and tie and rolled up his shirtsleeves in an unhurried manner while Patricia waited with her hands clasped behind her back. Turning her to face the several dozen observers gathered around the whipping post in the rotunda, he unzipped her leather dress and let it fall to the floor. Patricia looked down at her shoes and at nothing else as a blush tinged her cheeks.

She was clad in an exquisite black lace and brocade corset with a décolleté bra. This London bought waist cinch gave Patricia a ravishing figure, which was the primary reason she had agreed to be exhibited. He turned her around and fastened her wrists into cuffs, which he then attached to the post above her head. Everyone admired the sight of Patricia's slim but lush bottom when it was turned towards them. Michael dispensed with her gossamer-sheer black panties immediately, pulling them down and making her step out of them. Then he knelt beside her to cuff her ankles together. As he rose to his feet he ran his hand up the backs of her long legs, hosed in sheer, black stockings.

Patricia was glad that her back was to them, but then was horrified to note that the whipping post had been positioned in front of a multi-paned mirror, in which she was able to see the reflection of almost everyone watching the exhibition. She saw Jane Eliot staring at her with great absorption and Jane's Valkyrie of a lover staring jealously at Jane. She saw little Susan Ross, impossibly fresh and dewy from her college graduation, gazing with open admiration at Michael's well-defined torso as he took up a flogger to begin with. Patricia also saw

Damaris, safely seated on the granite thighs of William Random, who appeared to be enjoying the view. Damaris was looking at Patricia and Michael with interest, but her head was nestled against William's throat and William's hands were locked around the Puerto Rican girl's waist. No problems foreseeable there, thought Patricia, who now found herself concentrating on everything but what was about to happen to her. Hugo and Laura were watching as well, sitting together with glasses of champagne, thighs touching, occasionally whispering to each other and laughing. Hugo wasn't so bad, thought Patricia. At least he had apologized. It took a real man to do that. And it hadn't been a terrible spanking. Very hard, of course, but she liked that. Her bottom had tingled for at least a half hour afterwards.

Everyone became riveted when the whipping began, because it was a real one.

"Pay attention, Patricia," Michael told her, lashing her smooth, white, bare bottom in a way that made her immediately cry out with shock.

"Hey! What about my warm up?" she demanded, under her breath.

"You're getting a whipping, not a warm up," he replied, lashing her hard a second time.

"Ow! You can't start out that hard!"

"Do I have your undivided attention?" Again the whip came down.

"You have it!"

"Good. Let's keep it that way," he told her, continuing to use the flogger, but more moderately, though in six or eight strokes he was back up to the same intensity that had made her cry out.

"But, what did I do?" she whimpered.

"What didn't you do? We could start with this morning, or the first day of second grade. You're just bad, Patricia."

"I don't remember being bad on the first day of second grade," she mumbled into the whipping post, hiding her face behind her arm as he laid on harder. Now she was fully focused on the whipping in front of them all. She had to show them that she could take it. It was important they realize that she was the right one for him. She certainly couldn't imagine Marguerite holding still for this kind of lashing, nor the tiny Damaris.

Marguerite was indeed shocked at the way Michael was whipping Patricia. Dark, angry, red marks were beginning to blossom all over her taut, white bottom. Damaris also watched with a pounding heart, remembering the couple of nights when she herself had received almost as hard a thrashing from Michael Flagg while his wife. But she saw no tears in Patricia's eyes or anguish on her face. Instead, she saw a concentration of the kind one observes in athletes. It was a point of pride to Patricia never to say mercy.

Hugo enjoyed the whipping very much. He liked seeing the haughty Patricia take it and greatly approved of Michael's vigorous style of application. He didn't think it was too hard. But Laura Random, his companion, deemed the whipping unduly harsh. She herself remembered being caned to tears by Hugo the summer before in front of a group of people and how it had humiliated her. She had thought him cruel and insensitive for months. Finally, because she missed his attentions greatly, she had forgiven him and allowed him to win her back. After which it was pretty well understood between them that he would never discipline her so severely again. The punishment they now witnessed made her tremble with anxiety.

And yet, an hour or so after the whipping, when Laura ran into Michael as he leaned in the bay window of an alcove off the third floor stairwell, a painful stab of pleasure rippled through her as she recalled the severity of Patricia's whipping.

"What are you doing?" she asked, dropping down in the window seat, which overlooked the cliffs and sea.

"Just getting away from the smoke," he replied.

"Don't you mean avoiding all your ex-wives, fiancées and girlfriends?"

"Come on, Laura, be nice."

"I'd much rather be naughty," she flirted.

"Is that so?" he smiled.

"If not now, when?" she asked bluntly.

"Does Hugo permit you to play with other men at parties?"

"Permit?" Laura laughed.

"Oh? It's not that sort of relationship?"

"Well, didn't you just see him spank Patricia? Right outside in the street he did it!"

"Because of extenuating circumstances, that doesn't count," Michael had the conscience to inform her.

"What extenuating circumstances?"

"I asked him to do that. To distract Patricia. Do you think it worked?"

"Michael Flagg, how entirely unethical of you!" Laura cried, remembering how upset Patricia had been after the public spanking.

"Do you really think so?"

"Can I have been so mistaken in your character?" Laura stood up suddenly.

"Take it easy, Laura," Michael yanked her back down. "You don't understand what Patricia can be like. She's been torturing me all day about this party -- the ex-girlfriends and all that, yet insisting on going. I merely thought that if something happened which made her the center of attention, she'd forget about being jealous of the other girls and enjoy herself more."

"Ingenious," Laura got to her feet, "but somehow it falls flat. Excuse me."

"Not so fast, Laura dear," he captured her small white hand and patted it between his large ones. "Now, we're not going to share this insignificant, little secret with that Patricia, are we?"

"Why not? I think she has a right to know what a stinker you can be," retorted Laura, trying to break away.

"I'm sorry, I was being rude. You did say you wanted to play, didn't you?" In one fluid motion, he pulled her down across his lap and imprisoned her with a heavy arm across her waist.

"No! I've changed my mind," said Laura. "Let me up!"

"Now that I've got you in this position, I don't want to," he stroked her bottom through her tight, shiny skirt. This tender attention took some of the starch out of her resistance. She had dreamed about a real spanking from Michael for years. All of her girlfriends had played with him. Even her little sister. He was so tall, so fair, and so handsome, with the rock solid thighs of an athlete to rest firmly upon. His large hands melted her. "You can relax, you know," he told her. Then he began to spank her, long and hard on the seat of her skirt, until Laura was stirred by the heat. Before he pulled her skirt up he asked her permission. But once it was up and her bottom glowed through her sheer black panties, he assumed an authoritative tone.

"You're not mentioning the incident with Hugo to Patricia. Do you understand me, Laura Random?"

"Give me one good reason why I shouldn't."

"I'll give you a hundred and one," he told her and smartly began to smack her on the seat of her panties. After the full count he pulled the panties down, rubbed her bottom deeply, bent to kiss it and inhaled the heavenly perfume of her dewy sex.

"Will you keep my secret?" he asked again.

"You haven't yet convinced me that it's important to do so," she challenged softly, unwilling for the punishment to end.

"It's going to feel harder on the bare," he warned her, almost regretfully. She ground against his thighs, hardly sensible of the pain in her excitement at finally being handled and manipulated by Michael. The birthday spanking in Marguerite's shop years before and the one stolen kiss in his car, while William was away for so long, had formed the sum of their physical contact. Now, for the first time she was solidly across his lap, held fast by his huge hand, for the attentions she'd longed to receive from him ever since the first day they'd met.

"Laura, knowing Patricia as you do, can you really be indignant that she got one extra licking? After all, she was being a noisy, snotty brat, disrupting the meeting like that."

"Patricia deserves to be thrashed twice a day," Laura agreed, grinding dreamily against Michael's thighs. Her bottom was turning a deep, voluptuous shade of magenta under his hand.

"And so do you," he told her, bringing his hand down hard. She almost climaxed when he deliberately spread her cheeks and smacked her in between them. Then he spread her thighs and slipping his left hand in under her tummy, inserted one long, middle finger up into her vagina.

"Oh!" she cried. He continued the spanking in this manner until she succumbed to a thrilling climax about forty seconds later.

"That'll teach you to be a tattletale," he added.

After Michael restored Laura's clothes to their proper order, she climbed back on his lap the right way around and they embraced in the alcove seat for a long time, with her head in the crook of his shoulder and his hands clasped around her taut bottom. Laura was caught, thus luxuriating in Michael's strong embrace some few seconds later by her lover, Hugo Sands, who had just dashed up the stairs on his way to the playroom.

Laura recoiled from the displeasure in Hugo's eyes and jumped off Michael's lap with a feverish blush. Hugo continued on his way to the playroom without comment. When he got there he abruptly decided to take his leave of his host and depart for the evening. Laura followed him and said, "Are we going?"

"I am," Hugo told her and went past her down the stairs. Laura ran down after him.

"Hugo, wait!" she cried.

"Well?" he turned.

"Hugo, please don't be angry. What you saw just now was no big deal," she lamely protested.

"Oh?" he folded his arms and waited for her to continue.

"It was just a little post-scene cuddle. It never occurred to me that it wouldn't be all right to play with Michael tonight, especially after I saw you spank Patricia earlier."

"I see," said Hugo, honorably refraining from revealing his pact with Michael.

"You do?"

"Good night, Laura," he said, turning to go.

"Hugo? Am I not to go home with you tonight?"

"Go home with me? As though nothing had happened?"

"But nothing did happen, Hugo. I just told you --"

"Laura, there was nothing casual about the way I saw you grinding on Michael's lap," said Hugo bluntly.

"I was not grinding!" she cried.

"Well, whatever it was you were doing, it wasn't fitting."

"Oh, Hugo, you can't be jealous of me playing at a party!"

"Playing is one thing, necking another," he replied stiffly.

"Necking?" Laura laughed.

"I've spoken to you about Michael Flagg before."

"I didn't think the ban applied to party situations," she protested softly.

"I don't want to have a debate about this, Laura."

"But Hugo, Michael's been a friend for years. We've never gotten to play and I've always been curious. We had an enjoyable session. Was it so wrong of me to feel a certain amount of affection, even tenderness towards him afterwards? Aren't those the emotions playing ought to elicit?"

"What you're saying makes perfect sense, but we both know that it's sophistry. You've had a crush on Michael for years and I'm sure you allowed him any liberties he sought," he intuited. She dropped her eyes guiltily.

"I didn't think that it would make any difference," she offered.

"You mean so long as I didn't find out."

"Hugo?"

"What?"

"I agree that I was frivolous, but I meant no disrespect," she vowed sincerely. This simple declaration pleased but by no means satisfied Hugo. Encouraged by his softened expression she pressed this small advantage to add, "Please tell me what I should do to make amends for my error." Her air was so contrite and supplicating that his irritation fairly subsided.

"You should stop being so flirtatious," he suggested, in a tone that touched her conscience.

"But it's so hard to resist temptation," she explained.

"Are you saying you ever try?"

"No," she replied honestly. Her frankness brought a faint smile to his lips.

"You know, Laura, there are words for girls like you," Hugo murmured, resuming his stride.

"I remember a time you wouldn't have scrupled to use them," she observed, falling into step beside him.

"Well, love has taken its toll," he told her unselfconsciously.

She smiled and said, "Hugo, when I first met you, you were an insultingly cynical dom with ice water in your veins. But recently you've become so ... almost human."

"Yes. It's been a real job of work."

"I understand you even apologized to Patricia tonight," Laura said as they went out to his car. "I remember the days when you'd be as likely to chug wine from a screw top bottle as apologize to a submissive."

"Anyone can become rehabilitated, Laura."

"Hugo?"

"Yes, Laura?"

"I hope you aren't in danger of becoming too civilized."

Hugo gave her a look as he started his car, to which she returned such an impudent smile that he couldn't help but lean over and kiss her. "Just wait till I get you home, young lady," he warned her.

"What happens then?"

"Then you'll see how a civilized man deals with a flirtatious fiancée!"

They had driven half the way to Hugo's house in the woods before Laura had the nerve to echo, "Fiancée?"

"Don't panic, I believe in long engagements," Hugo soothed her. "However, you should know that fiancées are whipped much harder for inconstancy than mere girlfriends."

"The way Michael whipped Patricia tonight?"

"Hardly. You'd be screaming for mercy on stroke two."

"Then what kind of a whipping, Hugo?" she persisted, laying her head against his shoulder.

"Well, since you were courteous enough to assure me that you meant no disrespect, I think my belt will do."

As a grandfather clock tolled midnight in the hall, Sherman decided to retire for the evening to the well-appointed bedroom Anthony had provided for him. Since his suite adjoined Diana's, he supposed he'd hear her come in and finally go to sleep just before dawn. Sherman wondered again why he had come. He could feel Anthony and Susan deftly conspiring to assist his case, but obviously Diana was a capricious child. Sometimes she seemed tantalizingly accessible, yet her sexual ambiguity restrained him. If she really preferred women, dare he ever suggest a culmination to their play more in keeping with his own ardent temperament?

Sherman emerged from the bathroom wrapped in a towel as a knock came on the door. He stumbled to the door without his glasses and opened it to admit Diana. The petite brunette, by now quite flushed with the evening's activities, slipped into the room and locked the door behind her immediately.

"Why, Sherman, is that you?" she exclaimed, "What a glorious physique you've been concealing under those baggy trousers! And I don't believe I've ever seen you without your glasses before. I suddenly feel faint."

"Hmmph!" said Sherman stiffly, stumbling back to the bathroom for his glasses. "It's a bit late for flattery," he told her, tightening his towel around his flat stomach and going to the dresser to brush back his wet blond hair. Diana came and sat down on the upholstered bench, which fronted the cherry wood four-poster.

"Are you angry with me, Sherman?" Diana asked, almost hopefully. When he looked at her in the mirror she returned a mischievous smile. Sherman's heart contracted but he remembered Susan's sage counsel and stared back at her coolly.

"I'm annoyed," he told her bluntly. "I came all the way from New York in response to your invitation and did not expect to spend the night being ignored."

"But, I'm here now, Sherman."

"So you are," he said, discerning an agreeable uneasiness in her countenance. Perhaps she did care how he felt.

"I'm very sorry I neglected you tonight," she said, in all humility, yet unable to keep from examining the exposed torso of her future lover for the first time. When he saw her looking at him, as a child eyes a dessert cart, he felt encouraged.

"I'm sure you're not sorry at all," he told Diana, "you just feel like playing with me now so you'll say whatever it takes."

"Well, Mr. Cooper, if you feel that way about me being here, I'll just leave you alone to brood and have Dennis massage my feet instead. I've been in these heels all night," Diana stood up suddenly and strode into her room without a backward glance.

With compressed lips and sudden determination, Sherman

followed her and took the phone out of her hand, "You'll do no such thing, you selfish brat. Dennis has enough to do cleaning up after all the guests," Sherman scolded.

"I assure you, Dennis would regard the task of massaging my feet as a reward rather than a onus!" Diana declared haughtily.

"That does it. Come over here," he said, taking her by her smooth, bare upper arm and firmly turning her over his knee, using her vanity bench as a seat. "You're getting a good paddling."

Positioning her neatly and properly across his lap, he locked one arm around her waist and smoothed down her skirt over her round, little bottom. "Now obviously, you didn't need me here tonight," he said, spanking her a few times very firmly. "So why did you ask me to come?"

"Because I've missed you, Sherman," she hastened to reveal, turning to look at him.

"Oh?" this confession stayed his hand for a moment. Then Sherman carefully folded back the skirt and white nylon petticoat and began to spank her in a measured and deliberate manner on the seat of her silk briefs.

"It was very rude of you and Susan to leave the meeting hall like that without telling anyone where you were going!" The series of hard smacks that followed emphasized his point. When he finished her bottom glowed.

"I'm sorry," she softly rejoined, grinding her silky muff against his thigh.

"I think you did that just to irritate me, Diana."

"I was naughty," she admitted.

"Yes," he sighed, pulling down her panties to her knees.

"Oh!" cried Diana.

"Modesty, Diana? From the girl who ground against a whipping post in front of twenty people while Marguerite Alexander flogged her?" Sherman paused to examine the condition of her luminous bottom and was satisfied to find her only lightly marked with pink stripes. "Was it at least a hard whipping, Diana?" he laid his hand upon her warm, tender bottom.

"Not excessively so," she replied.

"Well, you two did look very pretty together, but I prefer you in this position," Sherman told her and then proceeded to deeply redden her bottom with the palm of his hand. Relieving his frustration with Diana in this way excited Sherman and she soon became painfully aware of his manhood pressed against her tummy.

"Ow! Sherman, stop! Your penis is too hard and it's poking into me," she teased.

"You're going to take this spanking seriously, young lady," he told her firmly, grabbing an oval wooden hair brush off the vanity with determination while at the same time shifting her weight on his lap to make her more comfortable. He then applied the back of the brush to her bottom ten times, fairly hard and fast. This shocked Diana almost to tears and she panted with emotion.

"This is what you need," he said, pressing the cool back of the brush against her warm bottom. She wriggled on his lap. "For as bad as you've been, I should spank you till you cry," he declared, remembering Susan's suggestion. Diana bit her lip and waited. As Sherman raised the brush she fantasized he was her husband. Under this illusion, the ten brush smacks that followed seemed even more poignant than the first and had an even stronger effect on Diana, whose rich imagination had transported her to her honeymoon night.

"Oh, Sherman, darling, would you like to take me?" she turned to look at him, her face aglow.

"Diana, you know I would," he turned her around on his lap and took her in his arms, forgetting all about making her cry.

"But, could you do it in the way I've dreamed about?"

"I could do it any way you like," he brushed her lips with his.

"Sherman, would take me forcefully?" Diana petitioned breathlessly.

"I would, but you'll have to explain what you mean," he encouraged her.

"I want to pretend I'm being had against my will."

"But why against your will?" Sherman instinctively recoiled from the unaccustomed role of ravisher.

"Perhaps because I don't know what's good for me," Diana explained. "In my fantasy, my husband is determined to teach me about sex, but I resist his will. He responds by taking me by force, then forcing me to come."

"I suppose you realize that I'm not accustomed to taking women by force," Sherman said, on the verge of becoming offended.

"I promise not to struggle in the slightest," she assured him guilelessly.

"I might tie your little wrists together, just to make sure," Sherman said experimentally.

"Oh yes, please!" she murmured her assent to this plan, grinding on his lap.

"Stop that," he scolded, smacking her bottom. "I'm fed up with you."

"Because I'm so perverse?"

"Only where I'm concerned. You seem to yield to others instantly."

"Oh, no! Never instantly."

"You're a perfect kitten with Anthony Newton I notice."

"Are you jealous, Sherman?"

"Yes!"

"You needn't be. We've never made love. He's only made me come. And in the most childish way. You're the one who will have my true womanly favors."

"Your fantasies are dangerous, Diana," Sherman seemed troubled by the violent role she'd assigned him.

"Not if you're the only one who fulfills them."

"I should punish severely you for being so reckless," he told her, parting her legs to insert his middle finger into her pussy up to the knuckle. He made her ride it until she almost came. However, he stopped teasing her just short of this and instead ordered her to strip naked.

"Take everything off?" she faltered. He folded his arms and nodded. Out of the dress and high heels, Diana appeared smaller, younger and much more vulnerable. "May I wear just two things?" she asked him.

"And what would they be?"

She handed him a pair of rubber tipped, silver nipple clamps which she kept in a lacquered box at her bedside. "Susan puts them on me sometimes and I truly love them," Diana confessed.

Sherman almost flinched when he attached the clips to the fully erect, rose-hued nipples, which surmounted her firm, peach shaped bosom, but when he heard her sigh of pleasure, and observed the contented smile which then adorned her face, he knew that she had not exaggerated their power.

Now that she was naked except for her earrings, nipple clamps and the pearls around her throat he commanded her to assume the all-fours position on the bed. Piling pillows in front of her, he unceremoniously pushed her down over them, in which position her bottom was thrust uppermost.

"Put your wrists together in front of you, Diana," he ordered, taking a white tee shirt from the dresser and ripping it. Tying her wrists together with the soft, cotton shirt was the work of a moment and Diana regarded him with breathless expectation. Finally he discarded the towel, which had girded his own loins and allowed her to observe, for the first time, the exact magnitude of his desire for her.

"Wondering how it's all going to fit into your tiny, little pussy, Diana?" Sherman got up behind her on the bed and casually rested his large, hard, faintly pulsing pink engine against her bottom while gently but deliberately parting her thighs, then her labia. Diana gave a little groan in response and attempted to assist him by arching her bottom even higher and spreading her legs apart wider. She wriggled and rolled her bottom under his cock until he slapped her hard and ordered her to be still. "You needn't worry," he assured her, "because I mainly intend to sodomize you."

"Oh!" she cried with genuine surprise, trying to turn around.

"Keep your head down," he ordered and insinuated the smooth, blunt head of his penis against her creamy vaginal slit until it was slick with her juices. Then spreading her labia deftly, he inched his cock inside her by slow degrees. Diana was so acquiescent, so wet and softly sighing that he nearly forgot that the objective was to convince her that she was being taken against her will. Yet he was reluctant to disappoint her in this, the only sexual request she had ever made of him. Also, there was the notion that if he let her down this evening, she might never allow him a second opportunity to impress her with his mastery.

"Four times you've put me off, Diana, but not tonight," he plunged in a little deeper with this phrase. Still she felt him holding back, even teasing her with his large cock. Pistoning in with a quick, shallow stroke, he succeeded in making her yearn for deeper penetration. He felt her open to him and attempt to engulf him more fully. In response he smacked her bottom sharply.

"You're too eager for a nice girl," he told her coolly. She sighed in such a way that he knew she liked the scolding.

"Stay loose and don't cling," he recommended. "Just let me get it wet." He injected one more inch into her velvet glove and at the same time spread her blushing bottom cheeks to completely expose her tiny rear aperture. "You'd better concentrate on getting very wet, young lady, because I can't be bothered trying to find any lube in the house at this hour and I intend to take your bottom in about three minutes."

He held her by the waist and penetrated her vagina a little more with each stroke, until he was smoothly pumping a full three quarters of his thickly veined erection into her slick canal.

"Your three minutes are up," he warned, smoothly reaching under her and pressed his palm up against her flat belly as he filled her gripping pussy with his cock.

"No," she protested weakly, "please don't take my bottom like that. You're much too big. I'll die. And besides, this feels wonderful!" Indeed, the smooth, firm driving of his cock in and out of her pussy had begun to send shocks of pure liquid excitement through her body, the likes of which she had never before experienced. She felt that she was truly being taken, and that surrender was sublime.

"I'm sorry," he said firmly, pulling free of her snug vagina and positioning his knob between her bottom cheeks, "but you need to be taken like this, to teach you humility." He pulled her apart and used his penis to lubricate her with her own copious girl juices. "And discipline," he added meaningfully, holding her open and pushing through the ring into her bottom. "No, Diana," he warned, "don't contract. I want you open. Do you understand?"

"Yes, sir."

"Resign yourself, Diana," he forced another inch of hard cock into her tight anal ring. "Before I'm done with you tonight, you're going to accommodate every inch."

"No, I couldn't possibly," she protested, only to be rewarded by a hard smack on either cheek. "Oh god!" she cried, clutching the pillows. Being spanked and sodomized at once was sexual splendor.

"Oh no?" Sherman now amused himself by alternately spreading her apart with his fingers, feeding his cock ever deeper into her bottom and spanking her cheeks hot pink. Diana pressed against the pillows in sheer abandon, tottering on the edge of climax every instant as the largest, hardest cock she could ever imagine nearly painlessly invaded her bottom.

"I'll teach you to invite me to a party then ignore me all night," he told her, beginning to pump her.

"I'm sorry!" she whimpered, scarcely able to catch her breath for panting and sobbing with emotion.

"You'd better be," he told her, giving her a smack. She was touchingly, achingly, throbbingly responsive to every dart and plunge of his cock in her bottom and small, convulsive spasms rippled through her tummy almost continuously throughout their first sex act.

"I hope you understand you're being taken," he said, causing her girlish climax to burst like the torrents of spring and bath her thighs with liquid pearls. It was all over for Sherman then too, her orgasm triggering his own.

Presently he pulled her against him on their sides and reached around to free her from the nipple clamps. Each one coming off elicited a groan, which let him know how sore her nipples had become. But when he began to untie the binding on her wrists Diana pulled them against her protectively.

"No, Sherman, I want to sleep in bondage," she protested, nuzzling back against him.

"Well, that was easy," Sherman thought, his face buried in her perfumed hair. "What in the world was I worried about?"

"You see how you were worried for nothing?" Patricia chided Michael as they undressed for bed in his cottage.

"I have to admit, you mostly behaved yourself tonight," he was pleased to agree.

"Speaking of well behaved, I don't believe I've ever seen a more courteous group of ex-attachments than yours," Patricia commented thoughtfully. "None of them seemed even mildly piqued at my presence at your side."

"That's because they're all well rid of me and they probably feel sorry for you," he replied. "Of course, none of them know how diabolical you are."

"They might find out, if I moved to Random Point."

"Oh? Are you moving to Random Point?"

"I can't go back to Boston and leave you here with all these girls. You're probably an inch away from fucking Laura as it is."

Michael was grateful the lights were off when he felt the color rise in his face.

"You're wrong about that," he told her firmly, "But I wish you'd move here anyway."

"Michael?" she tucked her gossamer clad body against his nude one in the big wooden bed. "That was an awfully hard whipping you gave me." He took this as a hint to pull up her gown and stroke her bottom.

"I had to get your attention."

"I don't think any of the women approved."

"Really?" Michael seemed surprised.

"Laura said it seemed unduly stringent."

"Oh, she and her sister are famous for being cry babies," Michael told her, remembering Laura's delicate whimpers as he'd held her across his lap earlier that night.

"Marguerite looked shocked as well," Patricia pointed out.

"Well, that's just because she's so protective of other women."

"And your ex-wife seemed stricken with compassion for me."

"She's a baby too," he explained.

"Still, it was a very hard whipping," she murmured, content that she had proven her point.

"Yes, and you are the only one who could have taken it and liked it," he granted, "however, let's not forget that you're also the only one who deserves it."

"And what do you deserve, for being such an alley cat?"
"You."

Chapter Five

Aurora

Laura Random planned to spend the first proper weekend of Autumn with Hugo Sands. But as she was packing her overnight bag in Anthony Newton's house, Hugo walked into her room distracted.

"I don't think you should visit this weekend, Laura," he told her, dropping into a chair.

"Did I do something bad?"

"No. It's just that some house guests are arriving and I don't know how you'll mix with them."

Laura looked hurt.

"Victor is one of my best customers, but he's also a serious European Master," Hugo explained.

"I'll behave, Hugo, I promise."

"Laura, what if he decides to humiliate his slave in front of us? Or, offers her to me? Or wants to use you? Victor can be that way."

"He's bringing a girl?"

"He generally does. And his manners towards women are appalling."

"He sounds horrifying, Hugo. Why have such a person as a houseguest?"

"I'll sell him things if nothing upsets his buying mood."

"I want to see the slave girl."

"If you come, he'll expect you to be the second slave girl."

"But I don't have to be, do I?"

"Masters from the old regime take things like that for granted."

"You just want to play with the slave girl without me in the way," Laura asserted, coming to sit beside him. Hugo smiled at her.

"No, dear, it's just that if he finds out that you're submissive, he'll expect you to behave submissively. And when you don't, you'll blow my sale."

"Hugo, why don't you just tell him that spanking is the only thing I'm used to. Then, if I annoy him, the most he can honorably ask is that I submit to a spanking."

"Victor isn't honorable."

"We could force him to be."

"I see this ending in tears," Hugo sighed. "However, if you think you really can behave yourself, I guess we can give it a try."

That evening, Hugo introduced Laura to Victor Kesselring as his fiancée, to insure greater respect. Laura met the tall, Swiss financier's gaze only briefly, as Hugo had warned her that trouble would come from prolonged eye contact. They were warm brown eyes, set in a cool face, with thin lips that barely smiled upon the introduction. He was handsome, but lacked vitality. Laura could not help but compare his lackluster mien to Hugo's more animated demeanor.

The slave Aurora was briefly introduced to Hugo, to whom the pretty, young blonde made a deep bow. Laura judged her to be in her very early 20's, about 5'4", with very fair hair that looked natural, a round bosom, slim waist and possibly ample hips under the sheer flowered dress and opaque under slip she wore. Dainty lacing espadrilles adored her pretty feet, completing an outfit which would have been better suited to a cruise ship in the tropics than a brisk New England day. Her eyes were pale blue and expressive, though she mostly kept them on the ground.

"And where did you find Aurora?" Hugo asked, once they were settled in the downstairs sitting room. Aurora moved towards the fireside at once, but her master briskly ordered her to kneel in the portion of the room farthest from it. Laura was shocked, just as Hugo had predicted and felt her heart begin to pound.

"I picked her up in Hollywood two days ago," reported Victor casually, disposing of his lean frame in a carved wooden throne chair.

"Excuse me, but may I use your powder room?" Aurora timidly asked Laura, who was just about to escort her to it when Victor

informed Aurora coolly that she could wait. The blonde girl immediately dropped her eyes and subsided in her chair. Laura felt a lump
rise in her throat and she rushed out of the room saying she would
bring coffee. In the hall she stopped and leaned against the wall,
unable to prevent two tears from running down her cheeks. These she
quickly dashed away and then proceeded to the kitchen. Here she was
soon joined by the girl, who had been sent to help Laura.

"Oh, great!" cried Laura, pushing her into the bathroom off the
pantry. When Aurora emerged Laura made her sit down by the
enormous, old kitchen hearth.

"Aurora what?"

"Milne," she smiled prettily at Laura and remarked on the beauty
of the old house and the appeal of its master.

"And what about your master? Don't tell me you enjoy being
treated like this."

"I'm new to the scene," Aurora explained. "But I do agree that this
trip isn't turning out the way I thought it would."

"Didn't you bring any warmer clothes?"

"No. I didn't realize it would be this chilly."

"Come upstairs with me while the coffee is brewing and I'll give
you a few things."

Laura took Aurora up to the room, which Hugo had given his guest
for her use and gave her a pair of cream Victorian ankle boots to
exchange for the insubstantial summer shoes. This operation was
preceded by Aurora donning a garter belt, matching panties and cream
lace stockings, during which Laura observed the smooth, voluptuous
contours of Aurora's thighs and buttocks with admiration, though the
young girl's bottom did appear to be slightly marked. Laura also
wrapped her new friend in a thick, Irish woolen sweater, with a fringed
collar.

"That will keep you warm," said Laura, fondly arranging it around
the girl's slim shoulders.

"Thank you!" said Aurora.

"What are you doing with that horrid man?"

"I'm told he's a very good player, but I can't get into some of the
head games."

"Like denying you permission to go to the bathroom?"

"That's bad," Aurora agreed.

"And not letting you sit by the fire?"

"I know," agreed Aurora, with tears forming in her guileless, blue eyes, "what's the point of being in New England at peak foliage if I'm to be treated like this?"

"Oh dear," Laura commiserated, "is that what induced you to come with him?"

"I wanted to go for long walks in the woods," Aurora explained.

"I'll take you!" Laura cried.

"He'll never let me go. He'll tie me up in the cellar, damn him!"

"If only it weren't for the colonial furnishings Hugo's put aside for him, we could all tell Victor to go to hell," Laura mused, gently taking a brush to Aurora's long hair.

"All of us? You mean your master isn't like Victor?"

"I used to think Hugo strict, but compared to Victor he's Danny Kaye. Come on, let's go down and bring them coffee."

While they were preparing a tray with fruit and cakes Aurora confided that she was a recent graduate of Berkeley, who had written her thesis on the Brontes. She worked as a legal secretary in the day and at a B&D club in Hollywood several nights a week. Ever since she read The Story of O and Frank and I as a teenager, she'd harbored submissive fantasies and had recently enjoyed living them out at the club. The brooding European gentleman downstairs had promised her a thrilling holiday back east. She had a week's vacation coming at the law firm and had leapt at the opportunity to travel to an area so rich in literary history. She had envisioned visits to the witch museum at Salem village and the home of Emily Dickinson at Amherst.

But she soon saw that no touring to suit her tastes would be included on their itinerary. That certain luster with which Victor had seduced her in the dungeon, quickly rubbed off in the light of day. She was told they would sojourn in luxury. She was not told she would be required to sleep on the floor. Aurora soon began to realize that he wanted not a companion, but a convenience, someone to use and abuse at will.

Laura was horrified. Here was a glowing, gemlike soul mate of her own, with a cultivated mind, in bondage to a sadist. This could not be allowed to continue. She would see that someone bought the furniture if Victor did not, but the stakes of offending him had suddenly gone down in view of the creature of beauty and light she'd be rescuing for a week of walks in the woods and fine literary conversation. Aurora was just Laura's type, thoughtful, gentle and responsive.

Hugo came out to the kitchen.

"What's going on, girls?"

"Take this out to Victor," Laura handed Aurora the coffee tray. When the girl had left them Laura explained the situation between their guests.

"I told you you wouldn't be able to deal with this," Hugo reminded her, examining the tray of small sandwiches and petite fours she had prepared earlier that afternoon for his guests. "This is pretty."

"Thank you. Hugo, she's a darling angel. We could stroll in the wood discussing the novels of Maria Edgeworth. But he'll lock in the cellar if I even suggest taking a walk."

"Don't worry about that. I'll get him over to the shop to look at the furniture in a little while and then you can take the little angel for a walk. Meanwhile, can I trust you not to go to pieces in front of him for at least another half hour?"

"Yes, sir."

"Good girl," he squeezed her waist.

Two girls quietly busied themselves serving coffee to the men. But each was aware of Victor's eyes on their every moment.

"Where did you get the boots and sweater, Aurora?" he asked.

"Laura lent them to me, Master," she replied, with her eyes on the ground.

"Gave them to her," said Laura.

"How very generous," observed Victor. "How do you thank Miss Laura?"

Aurora knew what he wanted her to do and immediately complied by going down on her knees to Laura where she sat and kissing the tips of her black high-heeled spectator pumps. Blushing becomingly,

Laura hid her shock at her new friend's servitude by affectionately stroking Aurora's smooth, fair hair.

"No, slave, really thank her," Victor recommended. Aurora blandly lifted Laura's daintily shod foot to obediently apply her tongue to the sole when Laura pulled back and jumped to her feet.

"I forgot the cream for the coffee!" cried Laura, dashing out to the kitchen while Aurora sat back on her heels, her heart pounding for Laura's sake.

"Tell me, Aurora," said Victor, in time for Laura's return with the cow creamer, "did you defy my order and use the bathroom just now?"

"Yes, Master," Aurora reddened. Laura's face also heated immediately but Hugo merely sighed.

"You know I don't brook disobedience, Aurora," said the Geneva banker in his London accent. "Assume the position at once."

Aurora did not hesitate to kneel, place her head on the floor, raise her skirt and underskirt and pull her sheer ivory panties down to her thighs, revealing to them all a creamy white bottom, slightly marked with small, purplish-red lash weals, from the last whipping at her master's hands.

Victor pulled his belt off and wrapping the buckle around his hand, drew back his arm without further ado and administered a dozen hard cuts to Aurora's bottom with the strap. These she bore pretty well, accustomed to hard whippings from working at the club and growing more used to his rough usage. Never the less, pants of distress began to escape her lips by stroke four. By stroke seven she had begun to sob. Unheeding, he finished the twelve count, then shocked Laura even more deeply by ordering Aurora to spread her thighs and thrust her pussy up for the next twelve. Now he changed his position in order to aim straight between her legs with the end of the harsh leather strap. The first application in this manner elicited a scream of electrifying volume in the discreet drawing room.

"This will never do," said Victor coolly, removing a handkerchief from his pocket and stuffing it into Aurora's mouth. As he raised her face to do so, they saw that it was drenched with tears. Laura turned to Hugo with such a stricken look that although he'd been taking some enjoyment in witnessing the discipline, he realized it was time to call his guest to order.

"Listen, Victor," Hugo said, "this is a bit advanced for Laura."

"We're not punishing Laura," said Victor, looking Laura up and down.

"I know, but it hurts her more to see her little friend treated like this then if we were."

"Perhaps I should punish Laura instead. I'm sure she's the one who tempted my slave to disobey me."

Laura lowered her eyes and said nothing, trusting Hugo to save her.

"If you restrict your correction to a spanking, I see no reason to object," said Hugo coolly. "However, I don't want my fiancée marked."

Content with this much, Victor triumphantly ordered Aurora to set her clothes to rights and kneel at Hugo's feet.

When Victor took Laura by the hand and turned her over his knee she did not resist. She was terrified he would exert the full strength of his arm, as he'd seemed to do in wielding the strap across Aurora's backside, but instead he only proceeded to give her a very sound spanking, which seemed no more severe than any she had received from Hugo or her ex-husband for minorly annoying behavior. When he released her she was flushed, panting and surprised. He regarded her with a superior smile. She backed away from him, rubbing her bottom through her skirt, ashamed at the excitement she now felt.

"Good!" said Hugo, "Now why don't we go and look at the pieces? The girls can amuse themselves until dinner."

And that was how, in a couple of moments, with the imprint of Victor's hand on her bottom and his face on her mind, Laura found herself alone with Aurora again. She took her immediately upstairs and showed her where she could wash her face and brush her hair.

"Didn't that hurt horribly when he strapped you between the legs?" Laura asked, perched on a vanity bench beside the blonde girl.

"Yes."

"Well, what did you think about that?"

"I didn't like it."

128

"But you took it. You were going to take twelve. Weren't you?"

"I don't know, Laura. I never have taken twelve like that. I can't tell until I try."

"Well, let's hope you never have to."

"It was very kind of Mr. Sands to stop the punishment like that. Why did he do that?"

"Because he probably saw that I was about to faint."

"He adores you," Aurora told her.

Laura smiled.

"You know, it's funny, but when Victor spanked me, he wasn't awful at all."

"He likes you more than he likes me because you're so nice and slim."

"You're slim."

"Not my hips."

"But that's womanly. Everyone loves an ample bottom."

To prove this, Laura took Aurora to Marguerite Alexander's bookshop where they found the proprietress alone and were able to communicate the details of Aurora's unjust captivity. Marguerite was instantly charmed by the unassuming submissive with the face of a Botticelli angel.

"I've played with Victor Kesselring," said Marguerite, after appraising the marks on Aurora's bottom, "and he can be a little rough. Would you like me to kidnap you and keep you with me for the rest of your stay on the Cape?" Aurora shivered with pleasure as silken strands of Marguerite's long russet hair brushed her bare skin and the striking bookshop owner placed a tender kiss on either exposed cheek before carefully pulling her panties back up.

"Oh, yes!" Aurora replied.

Several hours later Laura returned to Hugo's house alone and entered the downstairs sitting room like a guilty schoolgirl who had cut her afternoon classes. Hugo was staring out the window at the sudden violent rain shower, which had just begun, with a glass of whiskey in his hand.

"Where's Victor?" she asked apprehensively.

"He's upstairs taking a shower. Where's Aurora?"

"I left her at Marguerite's."

"You what?"

"We love Aurora, Hugo. We won't give her back to him."

Hugo said nothing for a moment or two as he tried to control his rising temper. He did, however, give her a look that turned her legs to water.

"I knew something like this would happen," he finally said, in a tone of profound exasperation. "Did I not try to keep you and Victor apart?"

"Yes, but that was before either of us had met that lovely, innocent girl. Surely Hugo, your heart goes out to her!"

"Laura, stop being so melodramatic. She's a creature of the scene. She works in a B&D club. Inevitably she would have met someone like Victor. It's better she learn how to deal with the type than have you girls protect her as though she were your kitten. Now what the hell am I going to tell Victor? That my submissive kidnapped his submissive?"

"He was going to dump her in New York anyway, Hugo. This way she'll get to spend a glorious week here with us before she goes back to L.A. I'll buy her return ticket myself."

"Laura, you had no business taking matters into your own hands like this."

"Hugo, I was going to bring her right back, but the more she told me about Victor, the more convinced I became that he's a monster out of an Ironwood book. We can't give her back to him, Hugo, not even for a night. He abuses her. You've seen it. He makes her sleep on the floor and kiss his feet. He keeps her cold all the time and barely feeds her. She hardly ever gets to use the bathroom and he makes her swallow absolute buckets full of cum! Oh, god it's so Dickensian!"

Hugo shook his head and sighed.

"Laura, you're fulfilling my prophecy as we speak."

"But, Hugo, don't you feel sorry for that poor little girl?"

"Right now the only poor little girl I feel sorry for is you," he said coolly.

"I realize that there are consequences to be faced," she replied with fearful resignation.

Hugo left Laura in suspense and phoned Marguerite, who had just begun to show Aurora her collection of corsets in her pretty attic dungeon. Marguerite was confident that she could handle Victor.

"I see him every Spring in Paris," she told Hugo. "And lately I've been whipping him. If you send him my compliments and invite him to visit me tonight, I'll take the entire responsibility for kidnapping Aurora and make him glad to let me keep her for my amusement."

"Do you like the girl that much?" Hugo was surprised at the impact this wistful young lady was having on Marguerite and Laura.

"I adore the girl and I also love Victor. This will be no hardship at all," said Marguerite with a pleasant note of mischief.

"Laura doesn't love Victor," Hugo remarked to Marguerite while staring at the guilty brunette.

"That's because she's so terrified of him she can't recognize his genius as a player," Marguerite explained, encouraging Aurora to try on a waist cinch.

"Don't you think that's a shame?" Hugo asked, deciding on Laura's punishment for meddling.

"Yes," Marguerite replied ingenuously. "She's limiting herself."

Hugo told Marguerite that he would send Victor to her after dinner and hung up.

"Marguerite will keep him busy until eleven or twelve, but what happens later, Laura? What happens when Victor comes home and finds he has no submissive to tend to his needs? What do I tell him?"

"You tell him that he can have yours," Laura replied with a sigh of doom.

Victor arrived back at Hugo's house at midnight as his host and Laura were playing chess. They looked at each other at the sound of the door.

"I want you to remember that you brought this on yourself," Hugo advised her sternly, rising to his feet to greet his guest.

Victor barely looked at Laura when he entered and accepted a glass of brandy from Hugo. Laura stared at the chessboard feeling her face grow warm as the men ignored her for several minutes. Finally Victor looked directly at Laura and said, "It appears that my slave prefers the company of women to that of her master."

Laura did not raise her eyes, but the deep blush, which suffused her cheeks at this remark, gave eloquent proof of her role in the rejection.

"And I am therefore without a slave tonight," Victor continued, just as Hugo had predicted he would.

"I'm at your disposal, Sir," Laura mumbled, without daring to raise her eyes.

"Good," said Victor with satisfaction. "Go up to my room. Remove you outer garments and kneel until I join you."

Laura left without looking at Hugo. She went up to Victor's room and stoked the fire to heat it well before his arrival when she was sure she'd be ordered as far away from the warmth as possible. Then she stripped down to a richly brocaded ivory satin corset and g-string with her highest patent leather fetish pumps and knelt before the fire.

Victor arrived in a brisk, harsh mood, ordering her not to look at him and rudely exposing her bosom. Looking down she noticed that her perfect nipples were erect and wondered how this could be. She realized she felt somewhat excited, mainly by the sheer novelty of the situation. She had angered a dangerous man and he was now about to punish her for it. And because she herself had provoked the situation, her lover, within earshot, would do nothing to stop it. "Where are the nipple clamps?" he demanded, slapping her breasts.

"I have none," she trembled in reply.

"Clothes pins will do."

"I... don't take clothes pins, Sir," she stated with timid resolution.

"Oh, really?" his tone was heavy with sarcasm as he paced restlessly, looking for items he felt he should have been provided with. "What else is unacceptable to slave Laura?"

"I beg your pardon, Sir, but I'm not accustomed to being treated like a slave, though I will do my best to please you."

"Magnanimous of you after you completely alienated the affections of my submissive," Victor's voice cracked like a martinet. Laura bowed her head deeper and did not reply.

"Fetch some equipment. Immediately," he commanded, sending Laura scurrying into Hugo's room for a selection of floggers, straps and paddles as well as leather cuffs, boat hooks and rope.

When she returned he said, "Is this all?"

"Have I forgotten something, Sir?"

"Yes, the ball gag."

"I don't take a gag, Sir."

"I see. And where is your collar?"

"I don't wear a collar, sir."

"Well, Laura, what do you do?"

Laura held her tongue.

"Get me a couple of dildos anyway," he briskly ordered, after which Laura blushingly fled the room again, to return with a plastic vibrator and a rubber dildo, which she lay alongside a jar of lubricant next to the whips and other items on the bed.

Five minutes after Laura went to join Victor, Hugo began to hear cries and sobs issue from the bedroom above. He paced the downstairs sitting room with restless indecision. The first sounds were those of a palm slapping flesh. Hugo smiled briefly at that. She certainly had a good one coming for the precipitous way in which she had behaved, though he himself couldn't ever recall eliciting such noises from Laura.

Then the sounds changed and Hugo heard a lash being administered. It might have been to her bottom, her back, her thighs, her breasts, or even the soles of her feet, knowing Victor. The verbal response was more radical now, with Laura's cries sounding almost like screams. She began to sob in earnest and never really stopped crying for the rest of the session. Hugo lit a cigarette and stared into the fire, thinking about how much good this would do Laura. She was a willful girl who had to be taught to listen to the advice of others. He had warned her about Victor Kesselring, yet she had to come over that day. He had tried to protect her, shield her utterly from the attentions of this cruel and careless dominant, but she had to tempt fate. And jeopardize his big sale.

Perhaps it was all for the best, Hugo thought. Laura would appreciate him all the better after a night with Victor. Victor was doing to Laura what Hugo would never have the heart to do. Victor punished solely for his own enjoyment, without regard for the pleasure of his submissives. Moreover, Victor was confident that the honor of serving him was more than enough to solace the pain of any slave. Of course Laura would be expected to service Victor sexually besides gratifying his sadism, but this caused Hugo less concern than the whipping. Being compelled to give Victor head might humiliate but wouldn't harm her.

The lashing lasted for a very long time. Whips and bodily targets were changed but the sounds of strokes and shrieks remained consistent. Half way through the hour Hugo's thoughts underwent a slow reversal. He almost wished he'd taken a spectator's chair at the punishment of Laura, not only to monitor the event but also to see his stubborn girl made to tearfully submit to a higher authority. Then the tumbler of brandy he was sipping softened him and he began to be afraid for Laura's safety. Hugo looked at the grandfather clock and saw that nearly 40 minutes had passed. It was then that the situation seemed to fall into an uncomfortable perspective. Laura had been sobbing violently almost the whole time. Why wasn't Victor giving her a break? Hugo chain-smoked and paced, wondering whether he should run upstairs and break it up. She would no doubt appreciate this greatly. But did she deserve the consideration?

Shouldn't she have to face the consequences of her actions, as she herself had suggested? Certainly she knew the word mercy, but he hadn't heard it so far. He told himself that if he heard her cry mercy, then and only then would he go and break it up.

The next sound he heard was that of a razor strop slapping against smooth, taut skin. Laura's cries were more feeble now, as though she were becoming numbed to the shock of such severe corporal punishment, or was too exhausted to respond with greater vigor to the continuous assault. Enough is enough, thought Hugo, striding across the room, and then stopping short. No, he couldn't do it. It would be utterly absurd. Victor would think that Hugo had gone insane if he presumed to regulate the manner in which he was disciplining a girl. He had to let the session finish. It was the only way to honorably conclude the Aurora episode. And if Laura exerted herself to please Victor, he might even make the furniture sale as well. So he stopped himself from going upstairs and forced himself to sit in a wing chair by the fire and wait.

When Victor returned to the lash, Laura's sobs pierced Hugo's heart. He looked at the clock on the mantelpiece. Victor had been punishing Laura for almost an hour now. By this time she might be marked. Hugo jumped to his feet, it suddenly becoming obvious that although mercy was a word she would not scruple to use with him, the onus she felt under to entertain Victor would preclude its use tonight.

However, half way up the stairs the screams of pain suddenly stopped and a blessed quiet descended on the house. Hugo sat on the steps and waited. Ten minutes later the door of Victor's room opened and Laura emerged, limp and dazed. Hugo ran up the stairs to meet her and immediately caught sight of her shockingly bruised bottom as she turned to pull Victor's door shut. When she noticed Hugo she immediately put her back to the door, as if to hide the terrific marking left by Victor's whip. Then she fell weakly into Hugo's arms and allowed him to walk her back to his bedroom.

Hugo locked the door behind them. Her face was flushed and streaked with tears. She pouted up at him but her eyes with soft with pleasure at being in his arms.

"Are you all right?"

"Yes."

"Turn around, let me see your bottom," Hugo said, and took a close look at the profuse red, blue and purple markings which criss-crossed a bottom that had been alabaster one hour earlier. "You'll have those marks for three weeks," he predicted.

"That's not sexy," she declared. "I look abused."

"Sorry you interfered?"

"Not if we get Aurora," Laura retorted with spirit, touching her very sore bottom gingerly. Hugo took her on his lap in the easy chair by the fire. "Oh Hugo, he whipped the soles of my feet so severely!" She showed him the pink bottoms of her feet, and then cuddled against him without reproach. "I was truly punished," she added, giving Hugo an immediate erection. "He wants to buy me from you. He's going to make you an offer tomorrow."

"That ought to be interesting."

Hugo got Laura out of the corset, put her in a cotton nightshirt and tucked her into his bed.

"Ow!" she immediately rolled over on her tummy and looked terribly unhappy for a moment or two. "I can't lie on my back tonight," she confided, pillowing her head on her arms. He got into bed beside her and took her in his arms. With her head on his chest he pulled up the nightshirt and lightly stroked her bottom. "I'm sore all over," she murmured, but this did not prevent her from grinding her flat tummy against his him. "You should see how rough he was with the toys!" she exclaimed.

"Should I?" he sat up to pull her gently across his lap, pulled up the night shirt and lay bare her bruised bottom.

"Yes," she murmured, twisting on his lap sexily. "He shoved one dildo up my bottom so hard that I just know it irritated me."

Hugo turned the bedside light on to examine her bottom. Delicately spreading her cheeks he noticed a light pink abrasion to one side of her anus, clear evidence of a rough intrusion.

"Is it all right?" she asked.

"Victor is an idiot," said Hugo angrily.

He left her a few moments and soon returned with a cool cloth and some antiseptic ointment, which he applied with great care. However, he could not fail to notice that in spite of the terrors of her ordeal, her sable Venus mound was dewy with excitement. "And you are a very honorable, if not prudent young lady," he added, again drawing her into his arms. She wriggled against him and felt his erection with pleasure.

"Tomorrow, after Victor leaves, we'll get Aurora back and you can show her how a gentleman dominates a lady," Laura said with some satisfaction.

"I wonder you can call me that when I let that barbarian thrash you," Hugo was still fuming over the dildo rape of Laura's bottom, which Victor had so carelessly performed.

"The only reason I'm wet is because I was thinking of you the entire time," Laura confided, grinding her muff against his thigh.

"What were you thinking?" he asked, pulling her on top of him and guiding his cock into her. She ground against him as he slipped up into her. Hugo fastened his hands to her waist.

"I was thinking that when I'm... stubborn, I prefer to be punished by you."

"That's because you know I'll only spank you," he told her, patting her bruised bottom very lightly. This however was enough to make her wriggle against him with pleasure. He slipped into her more deeply and they made love in this position for several minutes, his hands gently stroking her punished bottom, his hard cock filling her to the maximum depth, her creamy muff grinding against his groin, and her clit finally exploding into a blissful climax as he held her fast. Pulling out an instant before his own orgasm, he ejaculated against her satiny belly.

The following day Victor left Random Point without buying any furniture from Hugo. Laura was of course mortified that Hugo's predictions had all come true and humbled herself to him accordingly. Deeply shocked, by the light of day, at the way in which Victor had marked her, Hugo bitterly regretted his lassitude in responding to her cries. Had he only gone into the room the first time he thought of it, he might have saved Laura from a largely undeserved punishment and the brutal, senseless marking of her flawless skin. If this was the way Victor customarily treated his submissives, Laura had been fully justified in attempting to rescue Aurora from him.

"You poor girl," he said, again and again as he gently smoothed and kissed her bare bottom, upon which the bruising looked so harsh in the cool grey light of an overcast autumn morning. Laura submitted to be taken across his lap in order that he might massage the contents of a Vitamin E capsule into her black and blue cheeks. "I hate myself for letting this happen!"

Laura turned at this violent declaration of love with great surprise and pleasure.

"It was all my own fault," she reminded him. "You told me to stay away."

"No Laura, you were right when you said I never should have had him in my home. I don't want to belong to a petty, bad tempered, male dominant fraternity where every night is hell night for the women I care most about."

Laura wriggled on his lap, the massage beginning to stir her. "It was worth a whipping to hear you talk like this," Laura murmured.

That day Marguerite informed Aurora that they were going to visit an extremely wealthy gentleman in the scene who lived on the outskirts of Random Point, in a white house on a cliff overlooking the ocean. Marguerite did not tell Aurora his full name, but Aurora recognized Anthony Newton, the Broadway composer, immediately they were introduced.

She had been brought to serve tea and cakes in a classic maid's uniform comprised of a smart a knee length dress of grey cotton, white collar, apron and cap and black stack heeled maryjanes. Marguerite had told her that everyone she would meet in Anthony's elegant drawing room was in the scene and that she would receive a great deal of allowance for permitting some of them to play with her. Modestly and deftly, Aurora went about the room serving tea.

Two beautiful young ladies, one a blonde, the other a brunette, sat at a table by the windows overlooking the sea, playing Scrabble. The blonde, who was called Susan, was introduced to Aurora by Marguerite as the sister of Laura Random. The other girl, Diana, gave the make-believe domestic a lingering look that made Aurora blush.

Anthony looked up from the piano long enough to decide that Aurora was delectable, then he continued playing a new song he was working on with a smile. Aurora didn't dare approach him for fear of disturbing his concentration and went instead across the room to the only remaining occupant, a young man of cool and fashionable demeanor, who sat at an escritoire working at a laptop computer.

Introductions were made between Carter Webster and Marguerite, who extended her gloved hand to the young man, whom she instantly deemed irresistibly sexy. He wore a loose black suit and grey shirt without a tie. His skin was very white in contrast to his straight, black hair. Although civil, Carter did not appear to wish to converse to any great degree as he extended his hand in greeting to the striking red-head.

"Carter is doing the treatment for my show," Anthony explained.

Aurora couldn't imagine a cynical and sensational writer like Carter, who had recently made his name authoring post modernist gangster movies, even watching a light hearted Anthony Newton musical, no writing the screen play for one. But Anthony, who loved Carter's scripts and had discovered that the young writer was a Yale man, like himself, would have no other adapt his story.

Susan and Diana, who were visiting Anthony for the weekend, had yet to form a complete opinion of Carter, who seemed to them provocative but aloof. They had, in fact, spent the entire previous day trying his patience, teasing him and attempting to put him out of countenance. The fact that he was one of the hottest properties in Hollywood meant very little to the Vassar brats, it was his good looks and potential as a sexy dominant that interested them. The sophisticated Susan, who had been Anthony Newton's lover and confident for over three years, was not disposed to take the boy with the ponytail too seriously. Diana, on the other hand, thought Carter devastatingly attractive, especially because of his superior attitude. And yet none of them had the slightest notion as to whether or not he was in the scene, apart from the broad references to B&D in his films.

When Marguerite had called to explain about Aurora, Anthony had taken Susan and Diana aside to tell that that they were going to have a treat. Marguerite was bringing them a beautiful little submissive from Hollywood whom Laura had rescued from a dreadful master the previous day and who now needed allowance in order to fully enjoy her visit back east. She was to visit them as a maid and they were to feel free to treat her as imperiously as they found amusing.

"This could be your first venture into dominance," Anthony suggested to Diana, who flashed Susan a naughty smile.

"You mean I can have my way with her?"

"Within reason," he told her.

Choosing her moment carefully, Diana started something the second time Aurora came around to refill teacups.

"You clumsy girl," accused the sleek brunette, "you've sloshed tea in the saucer."

"I'm terribly sorry, Miss," murmured Aurora, her cheeks reddening instantly. She was used playing in dungeons, not drawing rooms.

"A drop has splashed on my new cashmere sweater," Diana pointed out the invisible flaw.

Aurora bowed her head in contrition.

"You seem careless and inattentive," observed Diana, standing up haughtily. "I think you had better assume the position."

No one in the room was quite prepared for the dramatic way in which the young girl interpreted this command. Exactly as she had done the day before in Hugo's sitting room, Aurora knelt, placed her forehead on the carpet, thrust her bottom in the air, flipped up her skirt and pulled down her panties, revealing her still somewhat marked, but extremely beautiful, ample, white bottom to every one of them.

Needless to say, this provocative display of her pristine, 22 year old charms left them all momentarily bereft of speech, particularly as she readjusted her pose to spread her knees and everything else in line with them as widely as possible for their inspection, as she'd been so stringently taught to do by Victor.

Anthony paused in his playing and sat studiously with his chin on his hand to give this vista his full attention. Marguerite, who initially covered her eyes with one glove, now peeked out at Aurora from behind her fingers and blushed for her sake. Susan and Diana looked at each other with genuine surprise then each valiantly fought to suppress a smile. Then they all looked at Carter, who sat staring with total amazement at Aurora.

Diana unbuckled her thin black belt, pulled it from the loops of her size 5 jeans and wrapped the buckle around her hand in order to use the end as a strap.

"That's how you assume the position?" Diana spoke coolly but caressed Aurora's bare bottom with a gentle touch.

"Have I forgotten something, Miss?" Aurora turned her head.

"Yes, you've forgotten a number of things, the first of which is modesty," Diana scolded perversely, because they had all been relishing the view of her daintily parted labia, her slightly spread bottom and full divided thighs.

"You can thank Victor for that," Marguerite hastened to defend

Aurora's dignity, for she had no idea of how sensitive the young submissive was and feared she might be hurt by Diana's sarcasm. "Her last master taught her that this was what was meant by assuming the position."

"I see," Diana stroked the beautiful white flesh of Aurora's bottom tenderly. "But that doesn't make it right."

"Shall I alter my position, Mistress?" Aurora asked.

"I think you had better, my darling," Diana told her, kissing each buttock lightly. "Perhaps a skilled master can whip you like that without hurting you here (Diana lightly stroked Aurora's damp blonde muff), but I won't take the risk." In so saying, Diana helped Aurora to instead bend over an upholstered hassock, with her bottom uppermost and her knees and heels on the floor together behind her. Now the presentation was more modest, to the great disappointment of both Anthony and Carter, but less daunting to the totally inexperienced Diana. Marguerite approved fully of the change and Diana's good sense in effecting it.

Now Diana swung her strap against her own palm, to test the sting of a stroke. She then began to administer the end of the belt to Aurora's plump, up thrust bottom. Diana had a particular affinity for the strap but had never been on this end of it before. Like most extreme beginners, she erred on the side of lightness, until Aurora turned to her and said with inexpressible sweetness, "Oh Mistress, I deserve to be punished much more severely!"

Diana, who herself could take a very good whipping, realized that Aurora could as well and drew back her arm to administer it. When the girls' eyes met a spark of true emotion was exchanged. For Aurora it was splendid to be chastised by a beautiful, cultivated young lady and she abandoned herself to the exquisite sensuality of the moment. For Diana, who fancied herself at least fifty percent lesbian, having a receptive, full-bottomed blonde Venus at her feet, prettily requesting a harder whipping, was sublime.

Now Diana flashed Susan a look, Susan with whom she was deeply in love and to whom she was constantly submissive. Susan was not a pale, corn silk blonde like Aurora, but a goldenrod, with wavy hair, immensely long. Diana wondered at that moment how irresistible her own petite mistress would look in this position. Susan stared back at Diana with a cool, ironic look in her eyes that seemed to say, don't get too used to this.

Now Diana let go and really whipped Aurora, bringing down the strap across her smooth, fair bottom dozens of times, as fast as she could, until she almost grew dizzy with her exertions. Aurora shut her eyes, held the position and whimpered towards the end with every evidence of pleasure mixed with shame. Everyone could see that Aurora was a true submissive and that Diana was wearing herself out. Anthony watched with an excess of enjoyment.

Susan felt disconcerted by the degree of energy Diana seemed able to call forth for this endeavor. Now that her friend had been given a taste of dominance, would she be willing to return to her former role as Susan's submissive?

Finally the whipping came to an end. Diana helped Aurora to her feet then told her that she was excused. The blushing and trembling girl gathered the tea things and exited, followed by Susan, who wanted to make sure that she was all right and ask her about Laura.

Aurora had paused in the hall and leaned against the wall, shuddering with a sudden flutter of excitement as the face of the handsome, dark haired young man with the laptop flashed before her eyes. He was the last one whose eyes she had met before exiting the room and it was difficult to interpret his look. Certainly there was a touch of disapproval in his expression, as much as to say, only a little slut puts on an exhibition like that, but there was also a distinct spark of masculine interest that seemed to add, if you were my girl I'd see to it you never had to go beyond our threshold for a whipping.

"Are you alright?" Susan asked Aurora.

"Oh, wonderful, thank you."

"Oh, good," Susan smiled and formally introduced herself.

"What a charming young lady your friend is," said Aurora.

"Thank you for being such a good sport."

"Oh, I thoroughly enjoyed it. And please tell Mr. Newton that I don't need any allowance. I'm staying with Marguerite and then your sister and Mr. Sands for the rest of the week and they've already gotten my return ticket."

"Don't be silly," Susan said, realizing why Laura had been so drawn to this girl. "Anthony is rich and he adores submissives. We can do a lot for you."

Later that day Aurora returned to Marguerite's house a good deal more solvent and with the voluptuous memory of her elegant strapping from Diana Stratton to set her heart aglow all afternoon. Everyone had been so charming, except that remote young man from Los Angeles who had smiled at her in a condescending way when they had said good-bye. He had seemed the one outsider in the group. The two girls, Susan and Diana, were obviously scene to the core, as she was. And Anthony of course, seemed not only the natural master of the house, but of the women in it, yet in the subtlest of ways. As Marguerite drove them home, Aurora expressed her thoughts on the men she had met so far in Random Point.

"Mr. Sands and Mr. Newton seem extremely nice to me."

"Well, my girlfriends and I wouldn't associate with men who weren't nice," said Marguerite.

"But you said you've played with Victor."

"Oh, so we're bitter against Victor, are we?" Marguerite smiled.

"How could I feel otherwise when I contrast his behavior and attitude towards me with that of the gentlemen I've met since coming to this town? I tell you, Marguerite, it's really caused me to reevaluate my place in the scene."

"Oh? To what end?"

"When I return to the Keep it won't be as a slave. It will be as a... switch!"

"I'm so glad!" Marguerite approved.

"And I'll never go away on a trip again with a man who doesn't smile."

Aurora's return flight to Los Angeles departed from Logan airport on a Monday afternoon and was so overbooked that she was immediately bumped to first class and found herself seated beside Carter Webster, who was also returning home.

Having been virtually snubbed by the proud young man on the

occasion of their first meeting, this circumstance of seating somewhat robbed from Aurora the joy at finding herself in first class. She had decided that he was too handsome not to be conceited, too successful not to be blasé and too distantly removed from the scene not to be judgmental about her role in it and all of these suppositions contributed to the general air of unease and extreme shyness with which the sensitive Aurora regarded her neighbor as he recognized and greeted her.

"Hi there," he said, with a faint and Aurora thought, somewhat superior smile.

"Hello," she said, managing a polite smile of her own.

"We were never really introduced," he said, "Carter Webster."

"Aurora Milne," she replied, shaking his cool hand briefly.

"That was quite a exhibition you put on at Anthony Newton's," he plunged in, saying exactly the wrong thing. Aurora merely colored and got out her copy of Diderot's The Nun, which Carter noted with interest.

"So, what do you do when you're not serving tea?" he laid a distinctly mocking emphasis on the last two words.

"I work in a law firm. And... at a club a few days a week."

"A club? What club?"

"I'd rather not say," she declared suddenly, although not knowing why.

"A night club?"

"No."

"Well, what then? A health and fitness club?"

"Of course not." Aurora almost smiled at the thought.

"A club where you serve tea?"

"I've never done so there before, but now that I have the maid's uniform, I might begin," she reflected candidly.

"Why won't you tell me the name of the club where you work?"

"Why do you want to know? So you can sensationalize and exploit B&D in even more your next film than you did in your last one?"

Carter was taken aback at her vehemence. "You don't approve of my work?"

"I think it's wantonly and needlessly sadistic."

"That's funny coming from you."

"You don't know enough about me to say that," Aurora told him, opening her book with the intention of reading.

"While cruelty is a part of life art will reflect it," Carter pointed out. "Just look at the book you're reading."

"You've read this book?" Aurora turned to him with sudden warmth.

"Have you gotten to the part yet where the nun's path is strewn with broken glass by the other sisters?"

"Oh, that was horrid! But didn't you adore the lesbian abbess?" Aurora asked breathlessly. Carter thought at that moment that he could easily adore Aurora if she would allow him to.

"So you hate my movies," he reminded her.

"I hate myself for liking them. None of your characters possess a grain of nobility or even common humanity, for that matter."

"Look, you can't apply morality to 20th century life. My scripts are realistic you'd rather live in a fantasy world."

Aurora shrugged and opened her book again.

"Tell me the club where you work."

"Why?"

"Because I want to come and thrash you for being such a critical little brat."

"You're a good detective, at least you write about them. If you really want to find me, you will," she told him coolly, not knowing where she found the nerve to do so, yet instinctively realizing that the harder she made it for him, the more he'd be driven to pursue her. At this point she was no longer sure that she disliked him. The initial distaste she had formed for him had been dispelled when he'd admitted to having read Diderot, but she still felt he did not respect her and that perhaps he was not to be trusted. He might simply wish to harshly humiliate her, as some of the gangsters in his violent screenplays did to their rebellious molls.

"Oh, I'll find you all right," he promised firmly, while studying her delicate profile as she bent her head to her book. "And do you know what I'm going to do when I do?"

"No, what?" she turned to him with wide blue eyes, really

interested at what he would come up with.

"I'm going to turn you over my knee and give you a good spanking for being so self-righteous."

Aurora blushed gratifyingly and then really did bury her nose in her book as a flutter of excitement stirred her heart.

Now he himself briskly opened his laptop and returned to work on the script he'd begun at Anthony Newton's house. Aurora thought then that she had perhaps misjudged Carter Webster.

Carter, highly piqued at her apparent lack of interest in him, punished Aurora by not speaking to her for the rest of the flight. Though he did take the liberty of looking at her while she slept. It was quite annoying to Carter that he was going to have to pay to come see her at a club for who knew how long before he could properly take her out and he wondered why she chose to treat him in such a manner. Surely he was intelligent, attractive and important enough to date. So why was she insisting he start their relationship as a client?

As they were debarking in the L.A. airport he made a modest overture that was quite devoid of warmth, for this little nobody had injured his pride. "Why don't you give me your phone number?" he asked as they walked towards the baggage claim.

"Why?"

"Because I think you're very cute and I'd like to get to know you better."

This statement was so totally unexceptionable that Aurora was momentarily stymied. Meanwhile he had handed her his card.

"Or, you could call me," he told her bluntly. She looked down at the heavy, calling card, with only his name and number imprinted on it, impressed that he was willing to trust her with it.

"I'll think about it," said Aurora slowly.

"Fine," he replied, affronted by her reticence to associate with him. "Good-bye then." He strode off to retrieve his luggage and she wandered out into the bright Southern California sunshine to get a cab back to Hollywood.

Carter Webster drove his BMW convertible back to his house in Malibu Canyon and listened with great boredom to the numerous

messages on his machine. Because he was who he was, women in this town pursued him continuously. All of them wanted something. The actresses wanted him to write parts for them. The writers wanted him to inspect and recommend their scripts. The groupies wanted to suck him dry just to find out if his magic was ingestible. Only the ones he had to pay never pestered him. They were polite enough to wait for him to call them. He had to laugh when he realized that of all the women who somehow or other wanted a piece of him, the hookers were the least offensive. Carter was quick to assign Aurora to this category, even though she only worked in B&D.

Aurora's lifestyle annoyed him and he did not understand it. He had overheard Susan Ross and her sister Laura Random discussing Aurora's sensibility in the warmest terms a few days before his departure. And it was obvious to Carter himself that Aurora did not have the soul of a pro. So why was she debasing herself? The possibility that she was simply an exhibitionist he found irritating, but even this was not enough to arrest his growing infatuation.

 He decided that, in the best tradition of the silver screen, she was forcing him come find her in her natural milieu, either to shock him into realizing that she wasn't his type of girl or arouse his protective instincts towards her. The only question was, how long should he make her wait? He had no hopes whatever of Aurora calling him. She might do so eventually, but he had read in her body language a languid quality. She would take the time to think the matter over thoroughly before deciding whether she was inclined to see him. He could grow old in the three or four weeks it might take if he waited for her to call him and Carter was impatient.

He stopped at the newsstand on the way home and picked up the Hollywood Star and New Reality to study the photos of the club girls. This was nothing new to him. He'd often examined the pictures and read the descriptions of the dungeons without being able to force himself to call the numbers and make an appointment to visit.

Carter Webster was 28 years old and as sophisticated as his education and place in the world had made him, yet it was not until the previous week at Anthony Newton's house that he had ever been made to come to grips with his own, carefully repressed sexuality. Being around the cheerfully perverse Susan and Diana had helped. It reminded him of his own college days; when he'd had the nerve to playfully spank his girl friends. Girls that age, unencumbered with the cares of the workaday world, were so sensual and naturally mischievous. Nowadays every woman he met had an agenda. And none of them were very much fun. It would be fascinating, Carter realized, to have a gentle and literate girlfriend with whom he could explore his most adventurous sexual fantasies.

The scene he had witnessed wherein Aurora had voluntarily raised her skirt, bared her bottom and all but spread herself to their view, he had relived a thousand times in his mind. But the thrill this had provided had nearly been eclipsed by the beautiful performance given by Diana and Aurora with the strap. To see this kind of thing in the flesh, after so many years of dreaming perfect scenarios, moved him to an entire reevaluation of his own lifestyle.

Why was he dating actresses? If Anthony Newton could feel confident enough to indulge himself like this, why couldn't he? For years he had never met a single woman into spanking, whereas this weekend he'd met five. It alternately confused and frustrated him.

He couldn't find Aurora's picture in the paper under the club staff listings. Sitting down with a phone overlooking the ocean he called the two clubs with the biggest ads first. He had no luck at the first. The second club was called The Keep. The young lady who answered the phone seemed tense when Carter asked for Aurora, because in general real names were not used in such circumstances.

"That's the only name I know her by," he admitted. "We met on Cape Cod last week."

"Hold on," the girl told him and went away to check with someone. When she came back she told Carter that she didn't think the person he was looking for worked there and hung up. Carter knew he'd found the right club.

The next day he called the club again and this time asked whether they had any blondes in their early twenties with ample bottoms who could take a good spanking. The girl who answered the phone that day was effusive in her praise of a young lady who worked there on Tuesday and Friday nights named Belinda. Carter was told that

Belinda was quiet and reserved, well educated and articulate, a perfect lady in every way, with an extensive fetish wardrobe as well as street clothes. He was further informed that Belinda could take heavy bondage and whipping, collars, hoods and masks, nipple clamps and clothespins.

"What about just a regular spanking?" Carter asked.

"Oh, Belinda lives for spanking. It's her favorite of all. She has five different school uniforms."

Carter booked an hour with Belinda on Friday night at nine and asked that she be attired in a white blouse and jumper, ankle sox and oxfords with her hair in a ponytail. He gave his first name for them to write in the appointment book for Belinda to see the following day when she came in. Then she would have three days to think about what was going to happen to her on Friday.

Aurora was fairly amazed when she arrived back at work on Tuesday and immediately saw Carter's name in the book. And he even wanted her in a schoolgirl uniform! The moment she finished reading the note the phone rang and Aurora answered it.

"Belinda?"

"Yes, who is this?"

"It's Carter."

"Oh. Hello, Carter." Aurora's face grew very warm.

"I've made an appointment to come and see you."

"I know. Thank you for thinking of me," she politely.

"I haven't been able to think about much else since a certain afternoon last week."

"Well, is there anything I should know about the session? I mean apart from the uniform?"

"Yes. I was going to give you an assignment for Friday."

"An assignment?" Aurora was intrigued, expecting to be asked to write an essay.

"Yes. I want you to read Pride and Prejudice."

"How charming," she said with a smile. "Of course I will!"

Carter hung up with a racing heart. He had noticed the change in her tone and felt that he had taken the correct approach. Now all that remained was to plan the actual session.

Finally Friday night arrived. Carter tortured Aurora by being fifteen minutes late but was then promptly punished by being told that all the dungeons were taken. Not a patient man, Carter asked Mistress Hildegarde what could be done, whereupon that obliging lady suggested Carter kidnap Belinda away from the club for a few hours of private play. A price was agreed upon and paid in advance and Aurora followed Carter outside into the balmy September evening air in something of a trance. She was glad that they weren't to play in a dungeon for the first time, yet she was afraid to be alone with him.

"Get in the car," he told her.

"Where are we going?"

"Never mind that. Why didn't you call me?" He opened the door for her and got in.

"Because you called me."

"I didn't call you until Tuesday. Why didn't you call me Monday night?"

"I suppose you're used to girls falling over themselves to get your number," said she with a hint of a smile.

"Don't be insolent. Especially in that outfit. Now be quiet and behave yourself till we get home."

Aurora felt a flutter at these words but also dreaded the possibility of a hard punishment at the hands of this self-composed young man.

"Unless of course," he added, "you have something sensible to say."

"Mr. Webster, have you've ever done this before?"

"Do you think that's a proper question for you to be asking me?"

"I beg your pardon," Aurora bowed her head.

"Whether I've done this once or a hundred times should be immaterial to you." Carter found his way to the canyon drive quickly and suddenly they seemed quite alone on the narrow, upwardly winding, forested roads.

Aurora saw that he was determined to be cross and refrained from replying to this slight. Higher and higher they climbed, ascending into ever more exclusive neighborhoods, until at last Carter took the steep, narrow turn off which led to his house, a pretty white washed villa, set in amongst the overhanging trees and with a dramatic view of the canyon and ocean beyond.

He took her directly inside the house, which was decorated in an austere Southwestern style. The well-balanced touch of a professional decorator was everywhere though the overall effect was more severe than inviting. The sparse, distressed furnishings looked particularly uncomfortable, though the pastel washed walls were charming.

While Aurora examined the main room Carter turned his full attention to the placement of a solid wooden chair in its center. When she saw what he was doing she realized that she would soon be forced to account for her behavior toward this important man.

With a pounding heart she observed him remove his jacket and toss it aside. Then he sat down. "Come over here," he told her.

Aurora hesitated but a moment then marshaled her courage and came to him.

"Over my knee," he said, pulling her down across his lap. "That's where you belong." Carter held her in place with one hand and smoothed down her grey box-pleated skirt with the other. "How old are you, anyway?"

"22."

"Is that all?" he stroked her firm, voluptuous buttocks through the skirt at length, which soothed and aroused her. "No wonder this outfit suits you so well. You're barely out of the schoolroom," he told her, deliberately using an 18th century phrase. "Did you complete the assignment I gave you?"

"Not as such."

"Not as such? What does that mean?"

"I've read the book before, but I didn't have a chance to review it before our meeting."

"I see," he left off rubbing her and renewed his grip on her waist. "I give you one small task to complete and you can't be bothered. Is that it?" Carter's hand came down hard, in rapid succession, causing her to gasp with surprise but not cry out.

She could feel at once that this would be a perfect spanking, hard enough to stir her, but with no sharp edges. His palm and lap were solid and the way in which he held her, with his hand curved around her waist, communicated his desire to protect and possess her. She had no idea of how long he spanked her over her jumper. It might have been two or eight minutes. She was content.

"Do you know why I asked you to read that book?" he asked, pausing to lift her skirt and expose a pair of oatmeal cotton panties sprinkled with bluebirds. Aurora would have enjoyed the smile, which the sight of these brought to Carter's eyes.

"I have two theories," said Aurora, looking back at him.

"Okay. Tell me the first."

"To prove to me that you're not a Philistine."

This sally did of course not go unrewarded and the charming printed panties soon became acquainted with the palm of Carter's hand. After several dozen good smacks, to accurately convey his annoyance at the insult, he paused with his hand on her very warm bottom and asked for the second theory.

"To instruct me on the folly of relying too much upon first impressions?" she replied, after catching her breath and putting back one hand to rub her bottom. "Ouch!"

"Yes. Very good," he approved, taking her hand away and pulling her panties down to her knees. Her beautiful, lush bottom had never appeared to greater advantage with its delicate hue of pink against the creamy white. All of the marking left by Victor had by now disappeared and the canvas before Carter was satiny smooth.

"I notice you're keeping your legs together these days," he remarked coolly, firmly separating her thighs a few inches and caressing their silken inner surfaces with his hand. Aurora whimpered at this unexpected attention and wriggled on his lap. "Well, there's no need to be modest on my account," he said, pulling her panties off and tossing them aside. Now he spread her thighs even more and caught a glimpse of her baby soft blonde pubic curls, which faintly glistening with her excitement.

"Tell me, Aurora, when you were being such a rude, unfriendly little girl on the plane, did you ever imagine that scarcely five days later you'd find yourself face down across my lap, getting a bare bottom spanking?"

"No!" she replied with all sincerity. "That is, not until you mentioned it."

"I'm afraid that for all your incivility you've earned a sound spanking."

"I understand," she bowed her head and waited with a thumping heart.

He gave her twelve hard smacks on alternating cheeks. When he was done her bottom was reddened more deeply, tending towards magenta. "Philistine indeed! I ought to take a hairbrush to you for that," he mused.

"Yes, Sir," she agreed.

"Very well, get up," he said, pulling her up. "Stand with your face to the wall and your skirt up until I return. And no rubbing," he said, positioning her against the terra cotta washed wall. He returned a few minutes later with a large, oval natural wooden hairbrush and pulled Aurora back across his lap.

"Did you miss me?"

"... Yes," she answered shyly.

"Do I perceive a softening of attitude? So soon?" he raised her skirt and bared her bottom again. Then he took up the hairbrush and began to spank her rather firmly with it. She took the hairbrush spanking very well and even arched her bottom higher to it. He took this as a cue to spank her harder, which he did for several minutes, with Aurora growing ever more excited by the warmth and the sting, and Carter becoming increasingly aroused by her little pants of pleasure.

Presently he noticed her darken from pink to red and guessed that if he went on any longer, she would probably become bruised. So he left off spanking her abruptly. But he continued to hold her on his lap, a small, slim waisted girl with the buttocks and thighs of a goddess. He even laid his cool cheek against her warm one and kissed it.

"I love your bottom," he told her, editing out the adjectives "plump" and "creamy" at the last moment, to spare her feelings. "Never lose weight!" he commanded, in sudden dread of her becoming his fashionable girlfriend and feeling it necessary to shrink her exquisite proportions from a size 6 to a 2. "Am I permitted to touch you?" he asked.

"Yes," she shyly told him, thinking how different he was from Victor in every important way.

He slipped a middle finger up into her creamy pussy and was delighted by its damp, clinging grip. Then he pulled it out and inserted it into her bottom. The effect was dramatic. Aurora squirmed as he manipulated her, grinding against him until an intense wave of pleasure vibrated through her entire sex and she came as beautifully as she had ever done in her young life.

Carter helped her off his lap, greatly encouraged by the progress they had made, whereas Aurora felt ready to sink through the planked wooden floor with shame at the abandon she'd exhibited. She actually hid her face in her hands so as not to have to meet his eyes, but he pulled her hands away.

"What's the matter? Still hate me?"

"No," she replied softly. "But, what must you think of me?"

"I think you're the most bewitching girl I've ever met."

Aurora smiled modestly, quite used to extravagant compliments after sessions. But was that what Carter was?

"Perhaps I've misjudged you," she said simply.

"Finally you say something sensible! But since we are talking about me, please feel free to extemporize," Carter folded his arms and waited.

"Well, quite opposite to what I had expected, you seem sensitive, kind and scholarly, all traits I prize."

"Yes. I could teach you a lot."

"Like F. Scott Fitzgerald and Sheila Graham?"

"Only not so alcoholic," said Carter.

"Well, what's the protocol now?"

"Well, you take me back to the club, or send me back in a cab."

Carter didn't talk much on the way back to the club, but now and then looked at her in a way she found hard to define. Finally, as he drew up to the house he turned to her and opened the conversation again.

"You still have my number, don't you?"

"Yes."

"Call me," he told her.

"May I write to you instead?" she asked shyly.

"Write to me? You're going to make me wait that long to see you again?" Carter wrote his address on the back of his card and handed it to her with some exasperation. Aurora dared to wonder whether she had found her true master at last. At the last moment before leaving him, she impulsively threw her arms around his neck and hugged him hard. Then she was out of the car and running up the walk to the white house with the picket fence he was to come to know so well in the following weeks.

Not used to relying on the mail to communicate with lovers, Carter was agreeably surprised at the speed with which he received his first correspondence from Aurora, which arrived on Monday afternoon. This meant she had written the note and mailed it on Friday night, after their encounter. It was written in beautiful script, with a heavy, expensive fountain pen, on thick parchment paper edged with a Florentine border of blue and gold.

It read, *"Dear Carter, Thank you for allowing me to write you. I am still in a daze from our scene. I hope that it was not an aberration which caused you to require me to appear before you in a schoolgirl uniform or use a hairbrush to correct me. For you hit on my favorite scenario.*

I must explain that in spite of what you saw at Mr. Newton's, that I am more naturally suited to being turned over a gentleman's knee in a study than I am to being treated like a slave in a dungeon. It was perfect when you assigned me P&P. I felt you understood me then and were the one who was truly fit to instruct me.

Because I am so young and inexperienced, I almost got in trouble recently by placing myself under the authority of a crude master. Ever since then I have been on my guard against a certain stamp of dominant. When I met you that first day in Random Point there was a coolness in your demeanor, which alarmed me, and this is why I offered you so little encouragement when we met on the plane. I was quite wrong about you.

I hope to be forgiven for misjudging you. I have enclosed my phone number. I live alone and don't have a boyfriend.
       Your obedient, Aurora"

Carter called the number she had written down but did not find Aurora at home, nor was there a machine to answer her phone. This annoyed him greatly and he resolved to punish her for this the next time they met.

Work and meetings occupied most of his time over the next several days, though by Wednesday he was once again able to call her. Again, she was not at home.

Frustrated Carter took himself on a whim to the club, though she was not to work there again until Friday night.

Aurora hoped that the mail would bring her a reply to her letter, but none was forthcoming the entire week. Another blow came on Friday when she arrived at the club at dusk and discovered that Carter had been there to play both the previous nights. Surprised and hurt by this intelligence, she asked Mistress Hildegarde to give her a full account of the visits, which had consisted of Carter doing sessions with all of the submissives and engaging all the dominants for tape-recorded interviews.

All of this research put Carter's interest in Aurora into a new and somewhat less than flattering prospective and she began to suppose that she was little more to the writer than yet one more Hollywood freak show.

Pressing engagements occupied Carter all of Friday and Saturday, but he finally phoned her on Sunday afternoon and found her at home.

"Why don't you have an answering machine?" he demanded at once.

"I do have one, but it's broken," she lamely replied.

"Well, how do you expect someone to be able to get hold of you?"

"People manage," she retorted, somewhat resentfully.

"Why don't you invite me over? I'd like to see where you live."

"All right," she said, and gave the address of the tiny guesthouse in Los Feliz.

Aurora spent the better part of an hour rearranging her little cottage and explaining to her cats the importance of the man who was to visit them.

When Carter arrived some ninety minutes later it was with a big, sleek answering machine, which he immediately hooked up for her, alongside her large wooden sleigh bed.

"You bought me an answering machine?"

"Sure."

"I see that phones are all important to you."

"Time is all we've got, Aurora and I'm a very busy person. I'll bring a laptop next time."

"I suppose you didn't think much of my letter," she said, without meeting his eyes.

"I only have it memorized."

This rejoinder made Aurora flush with pleasure, then a small imp caused her to remark, "How did you find the time with all the playing you've been doing?"

Carter raised an eyebrow at the spark of jealousy she'd unconsciously displayed but calmly replied; "I merely wished to familiarize myself with your environs and associates."

"To what end?"

"To determine whether the club is the right place for you."

"You feel this a matter for you to determine?" she didn't know whether to be angry or flattered.

"As you said yourself, you're young and inexperienced. You almost got into trouble not long ago. Remember? Did it ever occur to you that the trouble arose from working in that club?"

"What's the matter with the club?"

"Nothing, it you're partial to a good, old fashioned whore house."

"How dare you?" This was the last thing Aurora expected Carter to say about the club and was completely at a loss to comprehend his meaning. "We do pure B&D, not sex!" she declared haughtily. "Or did you make it your business to corrupt the girls with money and drugs when you came in on Wednesday and Thursday?"

"I don't mean whorehouse in the literal sense, Aurora. And no, I did not corrupt anyone with anything. However, just look at you girls.

157

Sitting around in your lingerie, waiting for the door bell to ring, being appraised by anyone who walks in, being shut up in a small, dark room with a stranger and having to please him by letting him whip you!"

"But, that part is romantic," protested Aurora. "And I never sit around in just lingerie."

"Honey, that's not the place for a girl like you," he said gently.

"But it's part of my education," she replied with a stubbornness he hadn't seen before.

"Did you ever wonder what it would be like to get busted?"

"I never do anything even questionable, let alone illegal."

"No? What do you call letting me finger-fuck you?"

"But," she faltered, blushing deeply with guilt, "that was in your house. And that was different. I mean, I had met you before and of course I know that you're not an undercover cop."

"I see, you very often doing things that are illegal or very nearly so, as long as you're reasonably that sure you're not with a cop."

"No! Look, perhaps I have let a real player touch me now and then. But that's all."

"And I'm sure any judge in the world would find your blue eyes and pure soul irresistible and let you off with a warning, but what about those angry street girls you'd get thrown into the holding pen with?"

"My god, Carter, what a horrible thing to say!"

"Harsh reality, sweetheart. I mean, I'll be happy to bail you out any time or place, but I'm just worried about what they'll do to you before I get there."

"You're just trying to scare me."

"How much do you make on a good week at the club? Your best week."

"Maybe five to seven hundred."

"Is that all?"

"But that's good!" she protested. "Next month I'll be able to take my first European vacation because of my moonlighting at the club."

"I'll pay you a thousand dollars a week not to work at the club."

"Would that make me your mistress?"

"Call it whatever you like."

"Why can't I just keep working at the club and you don't pay me anything?"

"Because Carter Webster's girlfriend would not be working at any damned B&D club," he told her with determination.

"I'm not your girlfriend that I know of, or anything like it," she pointed out.

"That condition is about to change," he promised, pulling her down on her own bed. A great deal of kissing and pulling off of clothes soon followed. Then Aurora considered that it was time to give him, who hadn't demanded it, the benefit of her well-taught submission and dared to pull his zipper down and release his long, thick, cleanly circumcised cock. Startled by his size she began modestly, by applying the tip of her tongue in feathery little strokes to the underside of his mushroom knob. Lightly cupping his balls in her hands and gently squeezing them as she licked, she leaned into the shaft with her freshly exposed, lily-white bosom. The graceful appearance of her small, perfectly round and cherry tipped breasts recalled to Carter a hundred classic portraits of fair haired nudes with this same shape, delicate to the waist and fuller below.

"I'll take her to Europe myself," he thought, "and show her how she's been painted and sculpted through the centuries." But aloud he said, "Do you know what I've been longing to do ever since I first saw you that day in Random Point?" he pulled her head away from his cock.

"What, Carter?" she sat back on her heels.

"Sodomize you," he said, gazing steadily into her wide eyes.

"You're too big."

"Let me try. If it hurts, I'll stop."

"I'm scared to."

"I'll tell you what, I'll fuck you for awhile in the regular way and you can ponder my suggestion."

Aurora did not for a moment scruple to reach into her bedside table and extract a foil wrapped condom to guard their act of love, nor did Carter resist this intelligent precaution. Putting her on her knees and bending her over several pillows, spreading her creamy white thighs and determining that she was wet with excitement was the work of an instant and soon he was inside her.

"Are you thinking about me taking your bottom?" he asked, driving into her deeply and hard, with his hands clamped to her dainty waist. Turning his head he caught a glimpse of them in the mirror opposite the bed and felt overwhelmed by her soft, pliant beauty.

"Yes, but, it almost seems too big for where it is," she protested.

"Oh, don't be such a baby," he told her. When she made no answer he added, "Perhaps another hairbrush spanking would make you comply."

He placed the palm of his hand against her tummy and found the exact angle of friction deep inside her necessary to spur his climax, for he had no objection to putting off the sodomy until next time. It would give them both something to look forward to.

Because he had been looking at them in the mirror he had noticed that the threat of another hairbrush spanking had caused a blush to suffuse Aurora's face. Indeed, she seemed to melt from that moment. Inside her she even felt warmer and wetter. Feeling his own crisis nearing and hoping for a simultaneous orgasm, Carter began quite deliberately to talk of taking her out to Caswell Massey's in Beverly Hills to buy a good, stout, English hairbrush.

"And don't think I won't turn you under my arm and try it out right in the store!" he warned her. "Just a quick smack or two while the clerk's back is turned should be enough to bring a real blush to your cheeks, or even better, a hot tear of shame to your eye. And then you'll have to stand beside me while she rings up the sale, wondering whether she's figured out just how submissive you are."

Combined with his vigorous thrusting, this speech was enough to bring on her climax, which soon triggered his.

"One thing puzzles me," she told him, a little while later, as she served him tea in her gaily-painted breakfast nook. "If you're in the scene, and I think you are, why don't you have a girlfriend in the scene?"

"That's you."

"I mean, why haven't you had one?"

"I didn't even know there was a scene until last week. I've been bribing call girls to let me spank them. But it's not the same thing."

"Why do you think Mr. Newton had me come in when you were there?"

"I don't know. Obviously he knew I was into it, but how?"

"Maybe Susan and Diana figured it out and told him."

"I felt like spanking them both, but I don't think I said anything about it."

"Did you have any literature lying around?"

"God, you're right! I'd borrowed a copy of Sadopaidea from Anthony's library and it was sitting on my bedside table the whole time I was at the house."

"What a nice place Random Point was to visit," said Aurora, pouring her new lover tea as he took her grey cat on his lap.

Shadow Lane Volume 4

About the Author

In Random Point, everything is linked to spanking and this is true for the author of the Shadow Lane novels as well. Eve Howard has been writing and producing spanking erotica since the 1980's, when she began freelancing for one of California's largest fetish magazine publishers. While editing *Spank Hard* magazine (as Lizzie Bennett) in 1985, she was discovered by the video producer Nu-West and offered a chance to perform in spanking videos. In 1986 she published the first Shadow Lane story and the following year formed the video production company Shadow Lane with her partner Tony Elka. The Shadow Lane novel series, originally published by Eve in serial form in her magazine *Stand Corrected*, was brought out in paperback volumes by Blue Moon books beginning in 1992. There are nine titles in the Shadow Lane series and Eve is currently working on Volume 10.

Since 1988, Eve has written, directed and produced over 140 spanking videos, the vast majority featuring the same male-spanks-female dynamic portrayed in her novels. Female-friendly and designed to make people feel good, rather than guilty, about being into spanking, Eve suggests an irreverent alternative to the all or nothing B&D subculture portrayed in such beloved classics as *The Story of O*. Many spanking fans have discovered the real life spanking scene by following the same patterns of social networking as described in the Shadow Lane novels. And for almost twenty years, Eve's company Shadow Lane has been one of the primary social organs of the real life spanking scene. She lives with her husband Tony and three cats in Las Vegas.

Reader Reviews about the Shadow Lane Series

"I've become addicted to the "Random Point" series so much that I can't wait until the next chapter. I've ordered the first two Shadow Lane volumes and have re-read them over and over. I never tire of them. Eve is the only person I know who can make an enema sexy."

"I discovered Shadow Lane about a month ago via AOL. Prior to that time I thought I could write excellent spanking erotica. Then I ordered, "The Problem with Laura." This is just a note to commend Eve Howard's spectacular talent and to say thanks for an incredible erotic experience."

"I have just completed "Return to Random Point" and decided that I had to write about how much I enjoyed it. I have not been so aroused since reading my first discipline novel many years ago, about a girl raised in England and "coming of age" as I believe they put it. More recently I have enjoyed reading Grant Andrews' My Darling Dominatrix and Ann Rice's "Beauty" series. It seems that women, though, have the right touch when it comes to writing about this subject. Eve, especially, knows how to touch that erotic nerve and bring it to a pure, raw sensuality until one feels that he/she is near bursting with lust."

"I, for one, have always loved (and by loved I mean devoured... breathlessly) Eve Howard's novelettes. To read them... especially when I was just 'coming out'... was to feel completely validated. I truly identified with each and every heroine; the feisty, sassy ones, the shy, demure ultra 'subby' ones... the young ones, and the more mature. I loved the gentle yet firm "taken in hand" nature of the romantic variety of spanking D's that Eve always incorporated into the stories. I loved that the plots were not complicated... but, feasible nonetheless. I loved the depictions of sexual escapades after many of the spanking interludes. I appreciated that the girls were cherished and adored by the affably rogue-ish gents... that the submitting was willing and desired... that it wasn't like 'rape.'

I like the settings... having grown up in New England and living here almost my whole life. I LOVED the idea of the bookstore (which I always find sexy). Then and now. I could cite many passages too, but I fear I've rambled enough. Eve was/is always my favorite spanking author."